Alstrom

Jane Retzig

Jane Retzig

With thanks to Heather LeAnn, and Naomi Rose-Mock for so beautifully bringing the voices of Alstrom to life in the music and audiobook of this novel.
And to Lesley, as always, for her brilliant editorial support.

The Music of Alstrom

is available on Spotify, YouTube, Apple Music, Amazon Music, and most other digital download and streaming outlets.

© Jane Retzig 2021
This edition 2022
ISBN: 978-1-7391002-0-9

This novel is a work of fiction. Names, characters, places and incidents are either products of the author's imagination or are used fictitiously. Any other resemblance to actual events, locations or persons, living or dead, is entirely co-incidental.

All rights reserved. Except for review, no part of this book may be reproduced in any form without permission in writing from the author.

Cover Photography – Nicolas Aguilera
Getty Images

One

SPAIN -27TH FEBRUARY 2019

Sixty five!

The thought wove its way into the dreams of Tyra Alström like a hosepipe filling and stiffening through tangled grass. She woke on the edge of crying out, with the remembered sense of a dark presence in the room. And she lay, for a long time, limp and sweat-beaded, feeling the thumping of her heart as she picked out the familiar things illuminated in the light that fingered around the edges of the window blind...

The wooden chair.

The wardrobe.

The desk.

And the simple bronze cast figure of Shakyamuni Buddha.

Nothing creeping or watching in the darkness.

Or at least, nothing more sinister than time.

Sixty five!

How the hell did that happen?

This impending day had hovered around the edges of her

consciousness for weeks. At first, she'd tried to push it to one side, working on the principle that if she starved the idea of energy, it would somehow wither and die. But a sixty fifth birthday isn't that kind of a thing. It's too significant. It had been too engrained in her consciousness for too long as the age when people retire. Of course, that age was edging upwards now across the globe. And Tyra wasn't eligible for a pension anyway. But even so, she had discovered that a birthday like this brought the spectre of old age with it. And much as she tried not to think about it, it filled her with dread.

Gingerly, she stretched her legs. The bed beyond her body was cold. And, as she put her nose out from under the covers, she could feel that the log burner had burnt out overnight, and the room was chilly too. This meant she must have slept late. She felt a rush of relief that she'd missed the morning meditation in the Shrine Room. And that, if her birthday was already well on its way, it was all the closer, thank God, to being over.

-0-0-0-

Later, standing at the door of the simple stone hut that had been her home for the past two years, Tyra looked out over the hazy line of the mountain tops. There had been a light snowfall overnight. But her hands were warm now, wrapped around a mug of strong Spanish coffee, laced with the familiar creamy smell of evaporated milk. She wore a thick, fisherman's jersey and lined jog pants. And, seeing one of the nuns walking by in her grey socks and hiking sandals, a black anorak unfastened over her maroon robes, she thought that she'd grown soft, living in these milder Mediterranean climes where winters was so much less harsh than the ones she remembered from her youth.

The nun had always thought that Tyra was a striking woman, and probably a bad influence. Her hair, still dark in patches, but mostly silver, was cut short, though not shaved as the heads of the religious were. It was tousled now, standing up in wayward spikes – uncombed. Her sapphire blue eyes had faded only slightly over time. There was something androgynous and almost ageless about her. Something tantalising. As if, according to the desire of the observer, she could be anything they wanted her to be. It was a quality she'd always possessed. And it had never served her well.

The nun avoided eye contact and hurried on, scattering flints of rock on the gritty mountain path as she went.

Watching her through the steam of her coffee, Tyra prodded cautiously at the idea that she was now sixty five and felt no different to yesterday, when she was only sixty four. It felt obvious that it should be so. And yet, it was surprising. And almost a little bit disappointing.

She wondered how to spend this anti-climax of a day. Certainly not meditating on impermanence with her fellow retreatants. This place had been a refuge for her. She loved the sound of the wind flapping at the brightly coloured prayer flags by the Stupa; humming in the rocks and crevices; teasing the windchimes hanging by the statue of Tara. She loved the drums and the bells and the singing bowls. And the low murmured chants of the faithful. Often these sounds would take on a rhythm and turn themselves into songs, with words forming in her head. She'd learnt to switch off when that happened, returning to the rise and fall of her breath as her teacher would direct her.

But she knew, even when she joined in with the community, that she would never really be one of them. Her heart had rarely felt at home. And it had never settled, even here, in this place of peace and beauty.

Suddenly, it came to her how she wanted to spend the day.

She pulled on her boots and jacket. Picked up her bag. And set off down the mountainside.

Two

La Nueva Casa was meandering gently through its sleepy village day. By the time Tyra had wound her way down the mountain, a cluster of locals were drinking red wine and eating tapas at the bar. The warm smell of garlic greeted her as she entered. A murmur of soft male voices paused then lifted again.

One or two of the men nodded to her. She nodded back gravely, always conscious that in any bar a lone woman who smiled and drank too much could be viewed as fair game. And she didn't want to be sized up by the old men. Or pitied by the young.

Mateo Paleo, the owner, had come to know her well. On her last visit he'd needed to enlist his son, Gabriel, to take her, on the back of his motorcycle, up the treacherous dirt track to the centre, and deposit her at the door of her cabin. But today, his son was with his girlfriend in the village. So, this time, he thought that if she drank herself under the table, he may just need to put a blanket over her and leave her in the bar.

Mateo was a kindly man. And he knew that Tyra was a

troubled soul. He'd heard rumours that she had been almost famous once. A singer tipped for stardom. And that drink and drugs had destroyed her. He thought, maybe, it was a good sign that he hadn't seen her for a while. But then, for all he knew, she might have crates of hard liquor at that stone cabin of hers, up there in the clouds with the monks and nuns.

'What can I get you?' he asked, addressing her in English. This seemed to be her language of preference, though he wasn't sure that it was her first. It was the one she lapsed into when she was drunk at any rate. And he wanted to head off her attempts at Spanish, which tended to give him the giggles.

Tyra took her lead from him. 'Could I have a carafe of red wine please?' she asked. She always started off slowly like this. Always believed, despite all prior experience, that she would be able to moderate the amount she drank. Someday, she thought, I'll reach that place where I feel ok and I'll just be able to stay there. But she'd never been able to do it. And now she was sixty five. A 'senior citizen'. And sayings about old dogs and new tricks came to mind. She swatted them aside. 'And some tapas... Gambas, patatas bravas, some olives... and some bread... por favor.'

Mateo observed her with deep brown eyes. Tyra always moved him with her clumsy attempts at politeness and her obvious discomfort in her own skin.

He thought that in her own way, she was beautiful. Not his type, of course. He loved his wife, who was black haired, dark eyed, olive skinned, and fiery. He liked a woman to have passion. To throw a saucepan at him from time to time. It added spice to a marriage to sometimes need to duck.

He thought that there was something about Tyra that seemed broken. All the spirit gone from her. It made him sad to think of it.

He poured a carafe of the house wine for her and placed it on the bar with a glass.

'We will bring your food to you,' he said gently, keen to get her out of stroking range of old José, who was looking at her rather too eagerly. The old man had taken to being a little too hands-on with the ladies. It had caused 'misunderstandings' on several occasions with female tourists.

'Maybe you would like the table by the fire. You must be cold after your long walk.'

-0-0-0-

Mateo was right. The fire was cosy. The smell of wood smoke and the crackling of the flames was hypnotic. Tyra half wished she'd thrown her good intentions to the wind and ordered spirits right from the start. The brandy here was good. She would order one when she'd finished eating. Part of her knew it would be the first of many. And she would have welcomed its glow from the outset, kickstarting her descent into numbness.

But for now, she would make do with the fire and the wine.

She looked around the room as she waited for her food. The building may be called 'The New House', but everything was relative in this ancient village, and she guessed that it dated back, at least to the late 1800's. It was plain; with unplastered stone walls painted the same white inside as out. Moorish tiles, in turquoise, gold, and navy, edged the fireplace.

The floor was wood and pitted with tiny burns from spitting logs and generations of cigarettes. And those same generations had rubbed the wooden tables and chairs shiny with their elbows and backsides.

In the small kitchen, through the beaded curtain behind the bar, she caught occasional glimpses of Mateo's wife, frying gambas in garlic. The smell made her mouth water as it drifted on a tide of Celine Dion through the beads from a radio by the stove.

Realising she was hungry, she took a deep gulp of her wine, feeling it warming her, and settling acidically in her stomach. She tried to distract herself by guessing what the men at the bar were talking about. Their voices were raised, so she imagined it was politics, or sport. Both were contentious issues here. Anything political ran the risk of raising tempers. But football was the hottest topic of all.

On the wall to her right, framed photographs of the Málaga CF football team, some autographed, were draped lovingly with blue and white striped scarves. To the left, in the interests of neutrality, photos of Granada CF were framed and displayed with the same reverence. Tyra suspected that Mateo himself supported Real Madrid, like his son, Gabriel, proud owner of the 1964 Triumph Norton parked in the cobbled alleyway leading to the rear of the bar. Gabriel Paleo proclaimed his allegiance proudly, with yellow, blue, and red ribbons streaming from the handlebars of his motorbike. But he was young and not so much of a diplomat as his father.

She looked up, startled by the sudden appearance of

Mateo's wife at her side. She was carrying the plates of tapas and looked gratified to have made her jump. Tyra hoped the surly woman didn't believe she was 'after' her husband. She smiled, trying to forge a link of female solidarity. 'This looks lovely!' she said. But the woman spoke no English and by the time Tyra had thought of the Spanish, she was gone.

Suddenly, she felt lonely, in this place where she was so clearly an outsider.

She knew that Madame Paleo would fight for her husband with a fierce unreasoned spirit if she suspected any woman of trying to win him from her. She saw how the walls here groaned with the passion of football supporters for their heroes. She thought of how the monks and nuns of the Retreat centre hung fine silk scarves around the necks of visiting lamas. How they showered the statue of Tara with offerings. She remembered how once she had been the minor object of that kind of adulation. How it had felt too heavy for her. And she thought: Everyone seems to worship something. Even if only money... Even if only themselves...

She looked inside herself to find what she revered. But all she found was a terrible sense of loss.

She took another long gulp of wine before she began to eat.

Three

By 4.15, Mateo was glancing anxiously in Tyra's direction. He thought she must be very drunk, though from his vantage point at the bar, she just looked sleepy. His regulars had drifted off to nap in front of their home fires. And his wife had disappeared upstairs, making shooing gestures towards their one remaining customer. La Nueva Casa habitually closed from 4 till 8pm, when the evening shift of drinkers and diners would appear. And sometimes on lucky days, Mateo would find his wife, not asleep and snoring, but waiting for him with the look of love in her eyes.

He was hesitating, tempted by the possibility of this, into simply dropping the latch and leaving Tyra to let herself out, or stay for the evening session, whichever she may prefer.

But then the door was flung open, and a young woman came crashing in. She was, maybe, in her early thirties. Her chestnut hair had darker lowlights and was layered down to her shoulders. She wore a black Berghaus walking jacket with straight legged indigo jeans and hiking boots that looked new. She had a rucksack in Day-Glo orange on her back. Tyra noticed all this about her. And, wondering if it made her a 'dirty old woman', she thought that if she'd been thirty years younger, this kid would most definitely have been her 'type'. She shook her head and laughed at herself as she focused back on her brandy.

'Phew! That was lucky!!! Just caught you!' said the newcomer, making a beeline for Mateo at the bar and stopping his 'I'm sorry we're just closing,' in its tracks.

She spotted his hesitation. 'It's ok. I don't need a drink or anything… Though I could have murdered a coffee.'

Mateo turned to the espresso machine. 'Con leche?' he asked, resignedly.

'Oh… seriously? Wow! You're a hero!'

She watched him as he steamed the milk and poured it into a shot of espresso.

'Thank you so much,' she said as he put the cup and saucer down on the bar. 'I was just wondering if you knew where I could get a taxi? I'm trying to get to the Retreat Centre up on the mountain. And the guy who brought me here didn't fancy driving up there. He said the track's a bit rough and he's not familiar with the road…. And to be honest, I think his exhaust was a bit too low slung for off the road motoring.'

Mateo shook his head. He'd understood the words taxi and Retreat Centre, and he'd just waved Carlos, the only taxi driver in the village, off for his siesta. Passing trade was rare here in the winter. And Carlos certainly wouldn't be awake (or sober) enough to drive the mountain track today.

Faintly, he heard his wife's voice from upstairs. In Spanish, thankfully… 'Mateo, what's taking you so long. Throw that old lush out and hurry while I'm still hot for you.'

'Two minutes, my sweet!' he called, also in Spanish, knowing it would be longer, but hoping she'd still be on simmer, at least, by the time he got to her.

He grimaced apologetically at the new arrival, who was now cradling the coffee cup in her hands. She looked hopefully at him over its steamy rim.

'I'm needed upstairs,' he said. 'But you're in luck. The lady by the fire is from the centre. Possibly she could show you the way on foot?' (And kill two birds with one stone, he hoped, if she could prevent Tyra from falling into a gully.) 'I will just latch the door and the two of you can take your time to finish your drinks'.

'Are you sure?'

'Yes... yes... of course!'

'MATEO!!!!'

'Coming my sweet!'

And he was off, through the kitchen and bounding up the stairs.

By the fireplace, Tyra chortled into her brandy. 'He's terrified of his missus,' she slurred. 'Must say, I don't blame him. She's a real dragon.'

The newcomer put her cup back on its saucer. She'd barely noticed the other occupant of the room before. 'I'm sorry,' she said. 'I feel like you just got lumbered with me.'

Tyra made a dismissive 'Pfft' noise to indicate that it wasn't a problem. 'S'okay... We can head up there when you've had your coffee. I'll just finish this.' She gesticulated at the half inch of brandy in her glass. 'Though I've probably already had a bit too much. Mrs Paleo obviously thinks so. She just called me an old dipso, or some such thing. I may not be able to speak very much Spanish, but I can usually understand it. Even when I'm plastered.' She chuckled again, then noticed that her companion had frozen, looking at her intently across the room.

'What?' she asked, suddenly overtaken by one of those 'What're you looking at?' fits of paranoia that go hand in hand with brandy and red wine.

The young woman took a sip of her coffee. She continued to eye Tyra over the rim of the cup.

Then she said, 'This might be a daft question. But... you're not Tyra Alström, are you, by any chance?'

Tyra stared at her across the room. Very occasionally, someone still recognised her. She had no idea how. Most days, she barely even recognised herself. She was so much older now, and greyer. But even when she was young and newly on the run from everything, she'd known how to camouflage herself well.

'Why?' she asked, defensively, just stopping herself in time from adding 'Who wants to know?'

'You are, aren't you?' persisted this suddenly rather threatening newcomer.

'What if I am?' There it was - more defensiveness.

The young woman took a step towards Tyra, who scraped backwards in her chair as if she might be about to make a run for it.

'I recognise you from your photos,' she was saying. 'I'm your niece... Elin... It's you I've come to see.'

Elin picked up her coffee from the bar, walked across the wooden floor and plonked herself down opposite her aunt.

As she came closer, Tyra could see what she hadn't noticed

at a distance. The resemblance, partly to her brother Peter, but more, much more, to Peter's wife, Helen.

And the name, of course. Elin. Peter's Nordic spin on naming the girl after her mother.

Her whole body felt like it was going into shock. And the room had begun to spin. She hadn't seen any of her family for decades. It was easier that way.

She hoped that she'd fallen asleep over her brandy and this was all some terrible nightmare.

But she felt her lips forming into a wan smile. She'd been conditioned to be polite, always.

She wondered if she should feel guilty that she hadn't been a proper aunt to this young woman... or her older siblings. It had been easy to neglect them when they were just names and grainy photocopied photographs in the formal newsletters Peter (who had also been conditioned to be polite) had written to her each Christmas. She'd sent cards and money for the kids, of course, until each of them reached eighteen. And dutiful thank you cards had come back to her. She struggled, even, to remember their names now. Elin was the youngest. And then there was Fred... And, slowly, it came back to her... Lucy.

'Dad gave me a letter to post to you,' Elin went on, in a voice that seemed to be echoing down a long tunnel. 'But I thought it would be nicer to come and see you in person.' In this place where everyone who spoke English, spoke it with an accent, Tyra noticed for the first time, the faint, familiar cadence of Sweden in her voice. It reminded her of her mother, who had died so long ago. And it made her want to cry.

She tried to focus on what her niece was saying. But she was distracted, trying to piece together the timeline of Peter's Christmas letters. At some point, she remembered, he'd uprooted Helen and taken her 'home' to Sweden. He'd had some crazy idea about returning to his roots. Musically. And geographically. The kids had been born there. Though, reading between the lines, it was just something else that hadn't worked out for him. She ran her hand over her eyes, trying to steady her gaze. She wondered if she was much drunker than she'd thought. Though she knew really that she was just afraid.

She sat helplessly, waiting to hear what had brought this stranger in search of her.

There was something in her niece's grave expression as she mentioned the letter that made her think it was going to be bad news.

Gently, Elin took a crumpled envelope from the front pocket of her rucksack.

She pushed it across the table to Tyra, who stared at it as if it may contain an unexploded bomb.

She recognised Peter's writing. Black biro. Her address. No stamp.

'I live near a Post Office,' said Elin. 'There aren't very many of those in England anymore. So, I tend to get lumbered with anything he can't just stick a first or second class stamp on.'

Tyra nodded, but she wasn't really listening. She found that she didn't want to open the envelope.

'What's it about?' she asked, dreading the reply.

'Grandad's dead,' said Elin, putting her hand on the table,

close to Tyra's in case the older woman might want to reach out in shock.

Tyra flinched away as if she'd been scorched and wrapped her fingers round the brandy glass like a child clinging to its mother's leg for comfort.

Thank God! she thought.

It felt safe to open the letter now. It was short and to the point.

Dear Tyra,

I'm sorry.

There's no easy way to say this. Dad's dead.

If you want to talk to me about it, you know my number.

Your loving brother always

Pete

Tyra folded it back into its envelope. 'Had he been ill?' she asked, mechanically, though she really didn't care.

'We don't exactly know yet. Dad found him. There'll have to be a post-mortem. But there's a backlog apparently. We're not sure whether he might have had a heart attack or stroke, or maybe even just slipped and banged his head as he fell.'

Tyra thought of her father. Bestselling author of Cold War spy novels. A long-running detective series. A trilogy about the SAS. Most of them made into movies. All action, no feeling. Isak Alström had been a sturdy man, proud of his robust health. She shuddered. It was hard to imagine the old tyrant dead.

'Dad's really cut up about it!'

'Yes, I can imagine.'

Peter had never handled stress well. She felt glad that Helen would be with him to help him through the trauma of it all.

'I'll give him a ring,' she said, feeling suddenly very weary. She hated talking on the phone. She hadn't spoken to her brother since she left England. And she really didn't want to now. But she knew that she should.

Elin looked relieved.

'Oh, brilliant! Thank you. I'm sure he'll be pleased to hear from you. And if you could maybe wait till tomorrow… And not tell him that I brought the letter myself.… I don't want him to think I'm interfering.'

Tyra nodded. She didn't imagine being on the phone for long anyway.

'And maybe you'll come to the funeral? We haven't got a date yet. But it's only going to be a quiet service at the church in the village. Just for family and friends. My dad says that's what Grandad would have wanted.'

Tyra smiled at her brother's small act of vengeance. Isak Alström would not have wanted a quiet service. He'd have wanted something ostentatious. Preferably at Westminster Abbey. With sobbing fans in attendance. And the 'A' list movie stars who'd played his heroes reading excerpts from his books.

'They're not going to inter him in Poet's Corner then?'

She said it with such a deadpan expression, Elin wasn't sure whether she was joking or not.

Tyra thought she'd better save her from deciding how to answer.

'You've come a very long way to tell me this,' she said, confusing her niece still further by changing the subject. 'Thank you. It was good of you.'

She was wondering what on earth you're supposed to do with someone who's just put themselves out to that extent. She felt torn. Part of her longed to be alone to digest the news. But part of her felt differently. That part wanted to cling to someone who reminded her so much of Helen. She felt discouraged that after so many years she could still feel like that.

Elin noticed that she hadn't said whether she'd come to the funeral or not.

She took a final sip of her coffee, taking care to leave the grounds in the bottom of the cup.

She took a deep breath.

'There's something else I wanted to talk to you about,' she said. 'And you may have already heard. But 'You Watching Me' is in the charts back home.'

Tyra looked puzzled. For a moment, she felt genuinely bewildered. It was so long since she'd thought of her old band, Alstrom, that she'd half forgotten the names of their songs.

The music charts?' she asked. 'Like... the Top Twenty?'

'Well, not quite that high. It's Number 35 this week.'

Tyra shook her head. 'I had no idea,' she said. 'How on earth did that happen?'

'It was the theme song for a Scandi-noir thriller... 'The Fördömelse Code'. It was shown on Channel Four.'

Tyra pictured the land of her ancestors. Of Elin's childhood, and her own. She'd been torn from those roots when she was nine years old because her father had never felt appreciated there. 'A writer has no honour in his own country,' he'd often said, misquoting Jesus. She'd been back, of course, with the band on a couple of occasions, and before, to visit her relatives. She pictured heavy skies. A landscape of blues and grey. And, from the few examples of Nordic-noir she'd seen, a serial killer. She could see how a song about her personal demons could echo the bleakness of all that. The music had been used without her knowledge. But she and Peter and the rest of the band had signed away so much when they were young and naïve and desperate, she had no idea who even owned their songs anymore.

'Dad was in the process of re-forming the band before Grandad died,' said Elin. 'He'd got Max and Danny on board. Turns out poor old Brian died last year.'

Brian had replaced Tyra on keyboards. He was part of Peter's master plan to keep her in the limelight as Alstrom's singer. Before Peter found him, Brian had worked in Woolworth's and played organ on Sundays at a Methodist Church in Battersea. He was older than the rest of them, balding, and with a secret fondness for Mills and Boon novels and cross-stitch. He lived with his mother in a flat near the power station. Tyra had always liked him, despite his unwitting role in Peter's manoeuvrings. He'd never entirely gelled with the 'Boys' though. They thought he was 'weird'.

'I'm sorry to hear that!' said Tyra. 'What happened?'

'I don't know. Dad didn't say.'

'That's a shame! He was a nice bloke.... Have they found somebody to replace him?' Tyra wondered if this was insensitive. Like in the old days when they used to shout 'The king is dead. Long live the king.'

'No. They're looking for someone. But Dad thought he could handle it in the meantime. He's heavily into synths these days. I think it appeals to his inner geek.' She rushed on. 'They've got a gig booked on the 3rd of May. It's just as the support act for a local band. But it's a start. And they were even thinking about recording some new songs. Danny's found some kid to stand in as a vocalist. But then this happened with Grandad, and Dad's gone into total meltdown. So that's the other reason I'm here. I thought… They've been looking for a keyboard player. And I know you liked doing that. And if you come home you might be able to keep Dad involved. I mean… after the funeral of course. It would do him good not to be brooding all the time. And to be honest, Alstrom's going to be rubbish without you anyway.'

It had been a long speech. Elin ground to a halt and looked hopefully at her aunt.

Tyra put her head in her hands. Her shoulders heaved. At first Elin thought she was crying, finally, about her father. She told herself it must have been the shock that delayed it and mentally berated herself for chattering on about the band. But then she realised, with a sinking heart, that what she'd taken for sobs were actually gasps of laughter.

Four

The day was slowly dying as they toiled up the mountain towards the Retreat Centre. Elin had assumed that her aunt would put her up for the night. And Tyra was surprised to realise that she was glad of the young woman's company. She also felt grateful that Elin clearly had no idea that it was her birthday. It saved them both the hassle of having to make a fuss of it.

It was a hard pull up the mountainside, and the track, used by walkers and an occasional fearless driver, was slippery with ice and small rocks. She was relieved that the steep incline gave her an excuse not to make small talk.

Now, she thought that if they made good time, they might get to her cabin before the sun had fully set. If not, she had a torch in her pocket to light the way. It was so often dark by the time she walked back along this lonely track, and the traditional heavy flashlight helped her feel safe. It served a dual purpose. Showing the way so she wouldn't break her neck in the darkness. And providing protection from any attacker deranged enough to come halfway up a mountain in search of victims.

'I'm trying to work out how old you must have been when you came back from Stockholm?' she said, pausing to allow Elin to get her breath back.

In the distance she could just make out the cluster of lights that marked the location of the ski resort. She knew that people would be hunkering down for the evening there now. The ski instructors and snowboarders would be taking on their night-time roles as MCs for quiz nights and party games. And brandy and red wine would be consumed by the gallon. She'd lived that life for a while after she'd left England. She'd moved around a lot back then, picking up casual work where she could find it. Here, and in Andorra and the Italian and French Alps. Anywhere, in fact, where no-one knew her.

Elin plonked herself down on a boulder. The cool mountain air felt like it was burning her lungs as she tried to breathe it in.

It was a while before she could answer.

'I was fourteen when we came back,' she panted. 'Lucy and Fred stayed in Sweden. Lucy had just embarked on her MBA and Fred was at the Royal Institute of Technology in Stockholm. He's a bit of a computer geek. And he already had his eye on Silicon Valley.'

'It must have been a wrench for you.' Tyra remembered only too well, how much of an upheaval it had been for her.

'Yes, it was lonely at first. But then I met my partner Dave, and he had lots of good friends, so I'm happy enough now.'

'Why did your mum and dad want to come back?'

'I don't think Mum did really. She liked the school she was teaching in. And she liked the life there. She had a lot of friends. But Dad never really settled like he thought he would.'

Tyra pieced together the sequence of events. Peter had played for a while in a Swedish Progressive Rock Trio. She guessed it may have been called a Supergroup if any of them had been famous enough. Sensing his excitement when he wrote to her the first year, she could have almost predicted that it would end in tears.

'So... the Swedish band lasted....?'

'Five years or so. And then he did some session work. And then switched to giving guitar and violin lessons. If he hadn't saddled himself with three kids, he could probably have managed ok on his private income. But I guess we were expensive. And he got into negative equity on property. And Mum's salary couldn't cover everything.'

Tyra nodded. Maybe she could have managed on her private income too. If only she hadn't had such expensive habits. Certainly, she'd managed ok in the past few years since she'd kicked most of them.

'And then along came this unexpected chart entry. And he thought he'd finally got his big break?'

'Something like that!'

Tyra laughed.

'How are Danny and Max?' she asked.

She thought of her two band mates. Danny with his dreadlocks and 'rollies' and mixed heritage; permanently stoned, and asleep, more often than not when he wasn't actually on his feet and playing his battered Fender bass. And priapic Max, their crazy drummer, all waist-length hair, tight jeans, and chiselled jaw. How they'd lived the rock star life in a group that, thanks to her, had never made it beyond the college and club circuit. Looking back, she thought she and Max had been like kids let loose in a sweet shop full of small town groupies and illegal highs. She shuddered at the memory of it.

Elin was still out of breath. She lived in Essex, where hills were rare. She enjoyed art galleries and good food. Her gym membership was festering in a drawer somewhere. And she'd expected to be able to find a taxi to take her up this nightmare of a mountain.

'Mum and Dad always kept us kids well away from Dad's rock band buddies,' she said, in a slightly raspy voice. 'I think they thought they might lead us astray. But they're both pretty keen, by all accounts'. Elin had a natural curiosity. Her parents regularly discussed things when they thought no-one was listening. And not much had ever escaped her. 'Danny has got his own little recording studio now. He works with disadvantaged kids mainly, and a few small indie bands. He had a heart attack a couple of years ago. But the docs put a stent in, and he'll be fine so long as he keeps taking his meds.'

'Still a stoner?'

'Not quite so much anymore. Not since the psychotic episode.'

Now Elin mentioned it, Tyra vaguely remembered something about that in one of Peter's letters.

'And Max?' she asked. She didn't remember Peter saying anything about him.

'He's a vicar now.'

Strangely, Tyra wasn't surprised.

'But he can take a sabbatical,' Elin added quickly. 'If things really take off with the band, of course. It's a bit of a 'don't give up the day job' situation at the mo.'

Tyra raised an eyebrow. 'Or ever, really,' she laughed. Then seeing Elin's crestfallen look, she added. 'Don't vicars retire anyway?' Surely Max must be close to retirement age, just like she was.

'Gosh, I don't know. I've seen some ancient ones.' Elin didn't want to get side-tracked onto the retirement age of vicars. Tyra's response when she'd first broached the idea of coming home hadn't boded well. But this interest in the others sounded more promising. 'It was like Dad had been given a new lease of life when he got back with the band,' she said. 'It seemed just the thing to get him back on his feet after Mum leaving. But then all this trauma with Grandad seems to have knocked him right back to square one again.'

Tyra's heart felt like it had stopped beating. She wondered if she was having a heart attack, like Danny. And maybe, like her own father. She felt cold and sweaty all at once. Her breath froze in her chest. 'What do you mean, 'After Mum leaving'?' she asked, at last.

Elin hesitated. 'Didn't you know about that either?'

'No.'

'I'm sorry, I thought Dad must have told you. It was before Christmas. She moved out in November. But things haven't been great between them for years.'

Tyra felt dizzy. She sat beside Elin on the boulder. The rock felt damp even through the heavy jog pants.

Elin reached for her, concerned. 'Are you ok Auntie Tyra?'

Auntie Tyra???? Jeez!!!

Tyra exhaled slowly. 'Yes, it's ok. I'm sorry. I just got a bit breathless! I'm getting old you know.'

She thought of Peter's formal Christmas letters. Polite enquiries after her health. News about the kids. Sweet anecdotes about the grandchildren in America, courtesy of Fred and his American wife, Brooke. There had been complaints about the band in Sweden and then about his hatred of teaching. She knew that she was meant to feel guilty about that. And sometimes she did. Peter believed he'd have been 'Living the Dream' if she hadn't messed it up. Not having to deal with 'idiots and time wasters' on a daily basis. And then, two Christmases ago, he'd shown a flurry of enthusiasm about his retirement, and she'd wondered if, finally, she'd been forgiven. But there had never been anything about any rockiness in his marriage. Never. Not even so much as a whiff of it.

'But why?' she asked. 'Was there someone else?'

Elin still felt concerned. Tyra had given her a fright. And she wasn't at all sure how she would get help if her aunt lost consciousness and left her alone, with minimal Spanish, and night approaching, on this awful, scary mountainside.

'They wouldn't have told us, even if there was,' she said. 'I guess Mum could suddenly shock us with a new toy boy. But I don't think so. I think she just got fed up looking after Dad all the time. But he doesn't do well without Mum. And it came as a bit of a shock to all of us really.'

Tyra stood up gingerly. She still felt dizzy, but she wanted to get home, make some toast or soup or something for Elin and get the fold-up bed sorted for the night.

She wanted to be quiet with her own thoughts.

Around the next bend in the track, she knew the gateway to the centre would be visible, shining in the gloom. The thought of that gave her the strength to go on.

Five

The interior cab light faded slowly on Elin as she buckled her seat belt. She'd hauled her rucksack onto the back seat and kissed her partner Dave on his stubbly cheek. They'd exchanged a few relieved pleasantries about the flight being on time. And they were conscious of cars behind, waiting to pull into their parking space.

Dave was not a confident driver. He much preferred walking or cycling, but he'd needed the car to take his mother shopping while Elin was away, and she knew he'd pushed himself way out of his comfort zone to ferry her to and from the airport.

She watched him fondly as he focused on following the exit arrows. He pulled up much too far away from the ticket barrier. And she tried not to laugh as he opened the door and scooted out of the car to post his ticket into the slot, frantically leaping back in, re-belting himself, and gunning the engine to get out, as if he were afraid the barrier would come crashing down and lock them into airport hell for all eternity.

They were both relieved when they were safely on the motorway and heading in the right direction for home.

'So,' Dave asked, relaxing a little now he only had to worry about the juggernaut drivers rumbling by as he stuck carefully to forty in the inside lane. 'Any joy with the mysterious auntie?'

Elin wasn't sure what to say about that. Certainly, her trip hadn't been as successful as she would have liked.

'I don't think she was particularly happy to see me,' she said.

'Well, she has been doing a Greta Garbo for forty odd years. So, I'm guessing you were a bit of a shock to her… How was she?'

'Hard to say… I found her in the bar in the village. She was pretty wasted.'

'Uh-oh! Wasn't that what caused the big bust up in the first place?'

'That's the official story.'

Dave glanced at her quickly before returning his anxious eyes to the road. He seemed reduced to a shadowy figure in greyscale as he clutched the wheel. Elin wanted to colour him in. Bring back his pale blue eyes, spikey red hair, and silver rimmed glasses. She longed to see him in the light of their cosy sitting room back home. It had been a tiring trip and she needed a hug. She sensed that he probably would too, after his driving ordeal.

'Do you think she'll come back?'

'I don't think so.'

'Oh!' said Dave. 'Right!'

They both lapsed into gloomy silence.

When they'd finally found the right junction and turned off the motorway, negotiated a roundabout, and started to head into more familiar countryside, Dave thought it might be safe to lift the mood. 'Is she still a cracker?' he asked cheekily.

'Hey!' Elin tapped him on the arm, rather more aggressively than she'd meant to. 'Don't you be turning into a granny grabber!'

He chuckled. He was lightening up now he knew where he was going. 'Well, she was quite something when she was younger…. It must run in the family.'

Elin eyed him suspiciously. Like a lot of attractive young women, she'd never felt confident about the way she looked. He'd paused just long enough for the final bit to sound like an afterthought. And now she wasn't sure whether he meant it or not. She decided to maintain a dignified silence on the subject.

It was starting to rain. Huge drops splattered the windscreen. Dave turned on the indicators, switched them off; switched his headlights to full beam; got flashed at; and hastily dipped them again. Then finally, to Elin's relief, he found the windscreen wipers.

'It's odd though,' she said, when he could see where he was going again. 'Dad has always said that it was Tyra who wrecked the band. Classic drink and drugs scenario. Messing up interviews, turning up late for concerts, generally screwing up. I mean, that's how it looked, isn't it?'

Before meeting her aunt, Elin had always believed her father's version of events. Her mother had never contradicted it. And there was evidence to back it up. Alstrom had boasted a small but loyal following. And many of the original fans were collectors. Over the years, Elin had amassed quite a library of recordings that at some point, had been converted to digital. There were a couple of bootleg concert tapes; an appearance on the Old Grey Whistle Test; and a short early local TV interview. The band had been tipped for greater success. But Tyra, like so many of her contemporaries, was, all too obviously, 'off her head' most of the time.

For as long as she could remember, Elin had believed that her aunt had single-handedly destroyed her father's dreams of stardom. But having met Tyra, she was no longer quite so sure.

'She didn't seem at all upset about Grandad,' she said.

'Well, I suppose if she'd cared about him, she'd have made the effort to come and see the old devil occasionally.'

'I guess!'

'And I can't say I blame her. He wasn't exactly the easiest of people.'

'He'd had a tough life Dave. There was the War. And losing Grandma like that. And then Tyra just buggering off and leaving.'

Dave sighed. He'd never liked Isak. He picked up creepy vibes from the man. Especially around Elin.

He knew it caused friction with his girlfriend when he criticised anyone in her family, but he couldn't help himself.

'And the international best sellers and film sets in exotic locations, and droves of fans to listen to him droning on endlessly with the stories we'd all heard about a hundred times before. Whatever you do, don't forget how hard all that was for him.'

'I think you're being horrid. You never liked him.'

'I'm sorry love, but I know his type. My dad was just the same. Total narcissist. He even made losing your Nan all about him.'

'Well, he was the one left to live the rest of his life without her!'

'Yeah... And your dad too, and your Auntie Tyra. I can't say I've ever heard him express much sympathy for either of them.'

Elin thought she'd better leave it. She and Dave had never seen eye to eye about her grandfather.

'I think something's gone on between Auntie Tyra and Mum too,' she said, eventually, when she thought the conversational dust had settled.

There was a pregnant pause while Dave thought about this.

Then, 'Woahay, two crackers together!' he laughed, spotting an opportunity to put the friction behind them by teasing her a little.

'Bloody hell Dave!' Elin hit him again. 'I didn't mean like that. God! Are you letching after my mum now?'

'Nothing wrong with that! They always say, if you want to know what your wife will look like in twenty years....'

'Was that a proposal?'

'If you like!'

'Well, I'm not having you. You've got a worrying interest in older women. And besides, I'm the youngest, remember. Mum was 35 when she had me.'

'Hah! Even better! I'll have something to look forward to in my dotage.'

Dave was still chuckling, enjoying getting a rise out of her. He took a rather too sharp left through the grim gates of the old Brentham Asylum. The grounds of the repurposed Victorian Psychiatric Hospital now held a small housing estate. There were neat rows of modern terraces, interspersed with larger, detached dwellings in the grounds. The original building had twenty luxury apartments and - as a condition of getting planning permission - five 'affordable' starter flats for local key workers. The place had a sad history, and it was rumoured to be haunted. But Dave, as a local lad, and now a teacher, had been eligible. And the pair had fallen in love at first sight with their one bedroom flat at the end of a long tiled corridor on the ground floor. It had a galley kitchen, and a cosy lounge, barely big enough to house their sofa, one comfy chair, and a TV, with patio doors leading to a small, fenced area where their French Bull Terrier Dido could lie out in the sun on good days. They'd been there for eighteen months and the novelty still hadn't worn off.

'Home sweet home!' he said, with some relief at getting them both back alive. 'Are you going to tell your dad that you've actually been to see Tyra?'

'I don't know.'

He gave her a sideways look.

'I know when you're up to something sweetheart. And I've been thinking about it while you've been away... You wouldn't be after writing a family biography, would you?'

Elin looked out of the side window. It was dark and the rain was coming down hard now. The clock on the tower of the asylum building told her it was only 7pm. But she'd been travelling for hours and she was tired. She thought of her father. His dreams and his dark depressions. About the brooding figure of her famous grandfather. She wondered about Tyra, who had been understandably suspicious of her, but had still given her a bed for the night and made sure she was delivered safely into a taxi the following morning. In short, she was intrigued by the unspoken stories that hovered around the edges of her family. Elin had a First Class Honours Degree in English. And her work as a freelance copywriter wasn't really what she'd had in mind when she'd embarked on it. She was bored, and longing for some outlet for her creativity.

'I might have been,' she admitted. 'But I doubt that it's going to happen. My family may have an entire plague-pit full of skeletons in their closets. But they're keeping their doors well and truly double-deadlocked for now.'

She pulled her jacket over her head to get out of the car in the rain.

'Anyway, let's get inside, I'm dying for a proper cup of tea.'

Six

Gate gate paragate parasamgate
Bodhi svaha

Tyra had been lost in her own world and only now found herself jolted back by the famous last words of the Heart Sutra. Those words had resonated with her even before she understood their meaning; pulling her back from decades of nihilism into a flickering idea that the emptiness she felt may not be such a bad thing after all.

Even now, after countless repetitions, she still had a fondness for them and she played them over in her mind as the elderly visiting Lama prepared to address the room, hitching his robes over his shoulders in the habitual, rather camp way of those who wore what was essentially a blanket in the middle of a Southern European winter.

Gone, gone, gone beyond.

Totally gone beyond.

So be it!

This was Tyra, translating the Heart Sutra in her own head. Not the Lama, who had no Spanish, and certainly no English. He sat to the right of the shrine on a throne covered in gold damask. His interpreter sat to his left on a folding picnic chair. He was a handsome young man with jet black hair shaved close to his head. Both men pressed their hands together and bowed their heads in greeting, beaming around the room with an innocent joy that would have merely seemed fake or cheesy in a Westerner.

All the room bowed back and settled, with much coughing and shuffling and every appearance of rapt attention, to listen to the words of the Master.

Tyra drifted off again. Shrine Rooms tended to have that effect on her.

This one was painted in the ubiquitous maroon and gold of the Tibetans. Candlelight tossed shadows against walls heavy with bodhisattvas trampling skulls or dispensing blessings. There was a calm feel about it, despite the fierceness of the 'Wrathful Deities' in the wall-hangings. And the whole place – even down to the smoky scent of incense - reminded her of the days when she hung out in bedsits with hippy chicks who fondly believed that their joss sticks would hide the smell of marijuana from their landlords.

She'd been something of a small-town celebrity back then and she remembered how women would touch her, all the time. How, when she was on stage, and knelt before them, they would reach up and tenderly stroke her, like lovers. And how afterwards, they would place their hands on her body as they spoke to her. How soft lips would come from nowhere in the haze of smoke and alcohol and brush against her own. And how someone, always, would lead her gently away to some quieter place where they could be alone. She'd feel then like just a body…. floating in a sea of sensation…. barely conscious that she was inhabiting some other woman's dream. But then, there'd be the morning, and the bleakness and regret. And a feeling she'd never quite been able to separate from grief.

She tried to be kind to herself about those days. But still, she cringed inwardly when she thought of them.

She remembered the last time anyone had touched her since she left all that behind. She wondered if that had been even worse than before. It had felt bleaker, somehow, without the drugs, or the defence of youth.

By the shrine, the Lama began to speak. His interpreter listened intently, then addressed the audience.

'Today, we will speak on the five principal afflictions… Attachment… Aversion… Jealousy…. Ignorance… and Pride…'

Tyra wondered if this enlightened one had somehow read her mind.

-0-0-0-

Later, back in the silence of her hut, she phoned her brother.

It was a bad connection. And their conversation was as stilted as she had expected it to be.

'Hi Pete, it's me, Tyra. I'm sorry about Dad.'

Now she was making the call, she realised how much Elin's request not to mention her visit would constrain her. She waited and hoped he would give her the chance to ask about all the things that really mattered.

'Thank you,' he said, flatly.

'What happened?' She wondered if a question could be classed as a lie if you already knew the answer.

'We don't know yet. It was probably a stroke or heart attack. I guess we'll get some answers from the post-mortem. But there's a backlog, apparently.'

Tyra remembered Elin saying exactly the same thing.

Silence stretched between them. She felt the sea and the mountains. And the years. And so many unspoken regrets.

'How are you Pete?' she asked, reverting to the Swedish pronunciation of his name. The way their mother had always said it. The way she'd said it, till they moved to England and had to fit in.

'Do you care... really?'

'That's not fair. And you know it!'

On the other side of the call, her words seemed to hit home. And when he spoke again, his voice was softer and less self-pitying.

'No,' he said. 'I'm sorry. It's been hard.' Then, 'Will you come home for the funeral?'

'I don't think so. It would seem hypocritical somehow.'

'Ok. I'll let you know when it is anyway. I've got your number now. I'll store it in my phone... If that's ok of course?'

'Yes, of course.' Tyra sensed that he was about to hang up. 'I heard that 'You Watching Me' is in the charts,' she said, suddenly not able to stop herself from asking.

His tone became suspicious. 'How do you know that?'

'I live in Spain, not Outer Mongolia.'

'Sorry,' he said, miserably. 'I'm not myself right now.'

Tyra thought, sadly, that this was very much Peter's 'self'.

Though it had never been a self that he'd felt comfortable showing to the world.

She waited to see what he would say about Alstrom.

'It was quite a surprise, I must admit,' he said. 'But I doubt there'll be much money in it. Not now everything's streamed.'

He said this as if she'd ever cared about such things.

'No plans to re-form the band then?' She couldn't help herself.

There was another long pause.

'I wondered about it, before Dad died. But I'm not up to it now.' He sounded edgy and evasive.

'It might do you good, you know.'

'Maybe…. Anyway, I'd better get off. There's lots to do, sorting Dad's stuff. I think there must be about sixty years-worth of junk in that old house.'

'Do you need any help with it?'

'No, it's ok. I've managed all these years without you.'

There it was again, the resentment. Tyra guessed it was so engrained now, it would never go away.

'Ok then,' she said. 'Take care.'

'You too!'

The line went dead. And Tyra thought he'd made it perfectly clear that, whatever Elin might think, Peter didn't want her involved with reforming Alstrom.

Seven

A FORTNIGHT LATER

Helen was in her old kitchen preparing a late lunch.

Since Isak's death, she'd taken to calling in on Peter to make sure he was okay. But the familiarity of the house felt threatening to her. She knew how easy it would be to allow herself to get sucked back into her old 'nothing really wrong with it' life there. It made her glad that her eldest daughter Lucy was due to arrive that afternoon to take over Peter-watch and give her a break.

It had been a difficult time for everyone. And a stressful week.

On Monday, the Coroner's office had decided they were happy to release Isak's body.

Then, on Tuesday, Peter had asked her to go into town with him to formally register the old man's death.

She'd been acutely aware that forty two years ago, they'd been married in that same Register Office. And part of her had wondered if he'd asked her because he wanted her to remember and feel wistful for happier times.

If that had been his intention, the move had misfired. The place didn't hold happy memories for Helen. She'd found it bleak then. And, sitting there, beside her not yet divorced husband, she wondered if it had ever been decorated since. It seemed frozen in some 1970's period drama. And the overwhelming smell of furniture polish and lilies had taken her straight back to that day when running away had just felt impossible.

Looking around the place in the present, she remembered details she thought she'd forgotten forever. Her mother in a pale blue suit and hat, unhappy that her only daughter was getting married here when she should have been married in a church. And her dad, who never could get rid of the coal dust under his fingernails, uncomfortable in the presence of Isak with his booming voice and big opinions about everything. Max and Danny had been there, in wide-lapelled polyester suits with flares, purple for Max and white for Danny. Brian too - surprised at his elevated status as 'Best Man', and overdressed in an outfit he'd ordered from Moss Bros. And finally, her best friend Bridget, who had made no secret of thinking that the marriage was a terrible mistake, but managing to put on an Oscar-worthy performance of being happy on the day. And nothing but a sad, heavy feeling of emptiness where Peter's mother, and Tyra should have been.

She realised now how young she was back then, and how alone, with all her secrets. Twenty five years later, for their Silver Wedding Anniversary, thinking that he was doing something romantic, Peter had framed one of the wedding photographs Max had taken that day with his Kodak Instamatic camera. Everyone had commented on what a lovely couple they were. But all Helen had been able to see was the sense of grim inevitability in it all.

Back in the present, she knew that Peter would have his own thoughts about their marriage. But neither of them had said anything as they'd sat side by side in the gloomy, oak panelled waiting room, each carefully avoiding touching, or mentioning anything about the vows they'd taken in that dreary place.

Not discussing things had always been their default position. It was easier that way.

And then today, Wednesday, first thing, they had been to the Undertaker. With a date and time for the funeral at last, Peter had handed Helen the job of letting everyone know.

And now she was making soup and a sandwich as if the last few months had never happened and she still lived here with him. Her hands were greasy, and the soup, in a pan on the cooker hob, had begun to seethe like a mini Vesuvius. She knew it would splatter all over the walls and cooker hood if she took her eyes off it for a moment.

Then the phone rang.

She cursed under her breath.

'Pete!' she called, hopefully, through the serving hatch. 'Please could you get that?'

Huddled in a blanket on a cane recliner in the conservatory, and with a phone handset clearly visible beside him, her estranged husband didn't move.

She tried louder... 'PETE! PHONE!'

Nothing.

She gave up, switched off the gas, and snatched up the

kitchen handset just catching herself from yelling into the mouthpiece.

'Hi,' she said, with the calm she'd usually managed to maintain in the years prior to her retirement, as Deputy Head of a rather challenging Essex Academy.

It was Elin. 'Hi Mum! I just picked up your voicemail. You sounded a bit frazzled.'

'Oh, hello sweetheart. I'm fine, honest. We finally got the Death Certificate for your grandad. We went to see the undertaker this morning and we've got a date for the funeral.'

Miserably, Helen noticed how easily she'd slipped into that 'we'. She knew that Elin would have noticed it too. And she hoped it wouldn't raise any false hopes in her daughter.

'Ooh that sounds rough. How's Dad coping?'

'Not so good. You know how it is! Anyway, the service is going to be on Wednesday the 27th. 3pm at St Mark's. Then just the family at the crematorium afterwards. And… Lucy's going to be arriving this afternoon and staying till after the funeral. Any chance of you and Dave meeting up with her at some point while she's in England? I'm sure she'd love to see you…'

They both knew she wouldn't.

'Oh… okay! Yes, of course. I'll drop her a text.'

Helen heard the flattened tone of her youngest daughter's voice. Lucy had greeted Elin's arrival in the family with tears and tantrums and things had gone downhill from there. There was no love lost between the two sisters. But Helen lived in hope that maybe, one day, they'd come to appreciate each other more.

'Look love, I've just made your dad some lunch, I'd better get it through to him before it goes cold. Are you and Dave ok? And Dido too, of course?'

Elin thought it was sweet, the way her mother always remembered her grand-dog.

'Yes Mum, we're all fine.'

'Good. We'll keep you posted about the finer details of the funeral.'

'Great. And don't worry about Lucy. I'll invite her across for tea. Dad too, if he'll come. And let me know if there's anything I can do to help…. ok?'

-0-0-0-

Peter wasn't asleep. 'Who was that on the phone?' he asked, as Helen set his lunch tray down on the table beside him in the conservatory. He brightened slightly at the distinctive smell of Heinz Cream of Tomato rising from his soup bowl. It had always been his favourite comfort food. One of the few things he really liked about England. He felt heartened that she'd cared enough to remember that.

'Which one?' she asked, wearily. She felt like she'd had the damn thing glued to her ear ever since they'd been back from the Funeral Director's. There were so many people to tell. Most of them had failed to answer and she'd patiently recited day, time and place to voicemail and told every one of them that they needn't phone back. But they'd phoned back anyway, and always when she'd just started to do something else. She'd noticed over the years that such things seemed to be governed by a mysterious universal law. You could wait all day for a call, or parcel, or tradesman to arrive. Then, the minute you turned your attention elsewhere, like daring to venture to the loo, for instance, you could guarantee, the bell would ring.

The calls had been difficult too. Everyone was worried about Peter, and all so used to her coping, that no-one but Elin had even bothered asking how she was. And Lucy, who had phoned in the middle of it all with her arrival time, seemed to have taken an almost malicious delight in being cool and offhand. She'd been frosty ever since the separation. But Isak's death had taken her to whole new levels. Helen had always tried hard to love Lucy. But Lucy had never made it easy for her, and she found her eldest daughter challenging. She felt glad she wouldn't have to stick around too long after she'd arrived.

'Was there more than one?' asked Peter, in a weak voice. 'I must have been asleep.'

Helen took a deep breath to fortify herself. 'Eat your lunch love,' she said, 'Before your soup gets cold.'

She waited until he had transferred the tray to his lap and taken a few slurps of the soup.

Gazing out at the yellow and mauve of the early Spring garden, she noticed that condensation was forming between the panes of the double-glazed conservatory windows. She was glad that wasn't her problem anymore.

'It was mainly people about the funeral,' she said eventually. She knew that once he'd got some momentum going, he would eat everything she'd put in front of him.

Peter had drifted off anyway. 'Do you believe in karma?' he asked.

'I don't know. I think life's pretty random, in the main.'

'You don't think people are punished then, for things they've done wrong?'

This was something Helen often wondered about when she was brooding over her own transgressions. She didn't want to go into any of that with Peter though.

'I think a lot of people are punished when they haven't done anything wrong,' she said, thinking of all the terrible things she read about in the papers every day. 'And some people do evil things and never get punished at all.' Like your father, she thought, though she didn't say it.

'But, maybe in the next lifetime,' Peter persisted. 'Do you think if someone has a guilty conscience it can make them choose to be punished?'

Helen laughed at this. 'I don't even think it has to be in the next lifetime,' she said, thinking of the kids at school and how some of them were incapable of allowing themselves to get away with anything. Elin and Fred too, would inevitably leave a tell-tale trail of crumbs if ever they raided the biscuit tin. Lucy, of course, had been a different kind of kid. She'd be more likely to deliberately leave a trail leading to Elin or Fred.

'Were you thinking of anyone in particular?' she asked.

'Not really,' said Peter.

But he looked shifty. Helen wondered if he was trying to guess his father's fate in the afterlife, though she knew he wouldn't be able to put any of that into words.

She felt suddenly very sleepy, as she always did when these great unvoiced chasms yawned between them.

'Lucy's going to be arriving at about 3pm,' she said. 'Do you mind if I go have a nap?'

'No,' he said, in a tone that suggested he minded very much.

She'd learned over the years not to indulge him when he was being like that.

'I won't be long,' she said, firmly.

She collected her own lunch on her way through the kitchen and headed upstairs to the sanctuary of the guest bedroom.

Eight

It was a relief to be away from Peter. And the room had always had a calming effect on her. She'd decorated it herself. Peter had never had any interest in DIY. So, at weekends, after Elin had become the last of her children to fly the nest, Helen had sanded and stained the floorboards. Then she'd painted the walls, sewn candy striped curtains and a bedspread to match, and found scatter rugs for a cosy finishing touch.

Increasingly, on nights when she couldn't sleep and Peter snored obliviously beside her, she'd retreated to that room to read until the early hours.

And it was there that she'd admitted to herself the full extent of her unhappiness and made her final decision to leave.

Peter hadn't made it easy for her. And she wondered, if she'd delayed, and seen his state after his father's death, whether she'd ever have had the courage to leave at all.

Sometimes she wondered what her life would have been like if she'd never encountered the Alströms. But, for better or for worse, she'd met Peter, and everything had been changed by that.

-0-0-0-

Their relationship started near the end of their first summer term of College. But she'd had a crush on him for months. He was handsome and endearingly tongue-tied. It had seemed odd to her that someone so desirable had been so lacking in confidence. And so alone. On the surface, he had everything going for him. He was tall, blond, and blue-eyed. He wore his hair long like Peter Frampton and looked a little like him too. He played acoustic guitar and violin and sang Donovan and Justin Hayward songs at open mic nights in local clubs and bars. In situations like that, where stage fright would have paralysed most people, he seemed to come alive. In the audience, where she increasingly manoeuvred herself to be, Helen thought that maybe, when he was performing, he could put down the burden of being himself for a while, and simply be a medium for something else. Later, in teaching, she wondered if she'd experienced moments like that. But she didn't think she had. Quite simply, Peter existed for music. And when he wasn't playing, or singing, or writing, he was lost.

Looking back, she realised how young they'd both been, and how naive. She'd had boyfriends before. One quite serious (at least, on her part) when she was sixteen. She'd thought her heart was broken when he told her he preferred another girl.

But Peter was different from the rest. She thought now of his questions about karma. Whether she had been punished all this time for pursuing him? For making him love her. And then, when it was too late, realising that she wanted someone else after all.

The first night they spoke, she'd deliberately 'found' herself beside him at the bar. Her friends had nudged her as another singer replaced him on the stage. 'I think it's your round!' they'd hinted, nodding in his direction as he wove through the crowd.

She'd been consumed by shyness. But his rendition of 'Nights in White Satin' had wooed her from the stage. And she'd goaded herself into asking, 'Can I get you a drink?' when she'd planted herself rather breathlessly at his side.

Close up, she could smell the sandalwood in his aftershave, and see the scars of his teenage acne. She'd noted the faint specks of dandruff on the shoulders of his black T-shirt and wanted to be the one to affectionately dust them away. Her heart had melted with tenderness for him. Later, she'd recognised similar feelings for each of her three children. But then, such a strong desire to protect was new to her. And it was easy to label as being 'in love'.

She'd felt horrified at her brazenness in approaching him like that. In 1970, 'nice' girls looked pretty, positioned themselves where they could be observed, and waited for men to come to them. He'd seemed surprised by her offer too. But he accepted and came back to the table where her friends were quietly amused at her success.

And later, when they'd walked back to the halls of residence where most of the first year students lived, those friends had conveniently melted away, and he'd kissed her tentatively, and asked if he could come in, knowing that it was unlikely that she would reject him.

He was her first lover. And she guessed she'd been the first for him too, though she never asked him about that. It had felt too important to make him feel that it had been 'good for her'. And it was. Her desperate need for him, stoked over weeks of longing, over-rode the starkness of the room, the single bed, and the nylon sheets. It over-rode his nervous fumbling, allowing her to lead him and show him where she longed for him to be. It made her feel strong and competent and in control.

Looking back at that night, Helen could see that Peter was depressed, even in the first flush of love. She'd thought, after the first time, that it was supposed to be the girl who cried. But at the golden dawn of the Seventies, his gentle gloom seemed romantic. She'd found a handsome nineteen year old poet who wrote songs about love and death and sang them to her shyly in her room. She was the envy of all her friends.

-0-0-0-

Peter had a summer job in Stockholm. His mother's family owned a group of upmarket hotels in Sweden, and he'd had holiday jobs there since he was sixteen. But for the start of the Christmas holidays, which also included his Birthday on the 21st of December, he asked her to come home with him to stay with his family.

Helen had felt excited and nervous all at the same time. Peter had often spoken about his mother and sister and it was clear that he adored them both. His mother, Kristina, had been a jazz singer before she married. She'd sung at the famous Nalen Club in Stockholm and hung out with Arne Karlsson the saxophonist, though Peter said his father didn't like to hear talk of that. His sister, Tyra was three years younger than Peter and still at a private girl's school near Cambridge. She played piano, and Peter described her as his 'best friend'. They wrote songs together, sending tape recordings and A4 manuscript sheets with squiggles and words, back and forth between them. This seemed unusual to Helen, but like most things about Peter at the time, she found it endearing.

The Alströms were wealthy. Their home, Renton Hall, just outside the village of Little Stockham, in Essex, was big, and dated, in part, to Tudor times. They had orchards and a summerhouse in the grounds.

Kristina Alström, Peter's mother, was a tall and strikingly beautiful woman, blonde, like Peter, and with a faint Swedish accent. She used the native pronunciation of her children's names, with an affectionate diminutive to each – Pieti and Türi - though both answered to English pronunciations everywhere else.

Mesmerised by Kristina on the first night of her stay, Helen thought that Isak, Peter's father, must have had supreme self-confidence to woo her. Peter rarely spoke of his father. And it was only when he asked her to come home to meet his family, that he admitted to her that he was, 'Isak Alström, International Bestselling Author'. He'd said the name and accolade all at once, and with such an edge of bitterness in his voice that, out of curiosity, she'd gone into W.H. Smith and sought out the glossy hard backed copies of Isak's latest book.

They weren't difficult to find, being stacked, several deep on a table with other new releases. They looked like the kind of thing her dad might read when he was on holiday. Not at all the sort of book that would interest her. But she'd been fascinated to see what Peter's dad might write. And she'd turned the book over in her hands, reading the blurb and author biography on the dust jacket. She'd seen then that he was not a good looking man. But in the huge oil portrait of the author mounted on the wall in the hallway at Renton, he appeared several years older than his author photo, dark and brooding, with a stocky build and unnerving stare. Helen felt that the artist hadn't liked him, though she admired the painting out of politeness when Kristina pointed it out to her.

As Peter was driving Helen home that first time, he'd explained that Isak was still away on a pre-Christmas book signing tour. Apparently, Isak Alström's books made popular Christmas gifts, especially for hard-to-buy-for husbands.

Helen couldn't help but wonder if her boyfriend had timed their visit deliberately, to ensure that it had the minimum possible cross-over with his father...

And maximum time with Tyra.

She'd seemed like such a sweet kid back then. Sixteen, and short and dark, like her father, but slightly built, with a mop of curly hair and the same stunning blue eyes as Peter and her mother. She arrived home at teatime on the 20th, a couple of hours after Peter and Helen. She was fresh from a Friday and Saturday night sleepover with a friend in Colchester. Peter ferried her assortment of cases and boxes from the taxi to the hallway, while she hurled herself first into her mother's arms, and then into the startled embrace of Helen, who wasn't used to such physical shows of affection, particularly from people she'd never met before.

'You must be Helen,' said the kid, before her mother had had the chance to introduce them. 'It's lovely to meet you at last. I've heard so much about you.'

This came as a surprise. Helen had always found Peter rather muted in his appreciation. But it was gratifying, none-the-less.

'I've heard a lot about you too,' she said. And then, before she could say anything more, Peter had put down the last bag in the hall. And Tyra had grabbed his hand to whisper, deliberately loud enough for Helen to hear, 'She's lovely Pete, just like you said.'

-0-0-0-

For Helen, from a mining village near Rotherham, the whole Alström experience felt strange and exotic, and somehow frozen in time, like something written by E.M. Forster, or Evelyn Waugh. There was laughter. And a sharing of light, affectionate touch that Helen had never known with her own family. She watched in amazement that first night as Tyra snuggled on the hearth rug against her mother's knees in front of the fire, and as Peter wrapped his arms around Kristina or Tyra's shoulders from behind, drawing them to him and kissing their heads mischievously as they worked together in the kitchen.

And there seemed to be so much to talk about. So many things to catch up on.

Tyra had played piano at the Carol Service at her school…

How had it gone? And Peter's last gig?.... What songs did he chose? Would he play them tomorrow for his birthday?.... How did Helen's family spend Christmas? …. Did extended family come to stay?.... How was old Mrs Hunter in the village since her gall bladder operation?... Was the vicar still planning to move to an urban parish?

Coming from a family of few words, Helen was new to conversation that wove seamlessly from topic to topic, the spotlight moving effortlessly from one person to the next as if guided by an unseen hand. And she was puzzled by a room with no TV set. She wondered if it may be hidden in the cabinet by the side of the fireplace, but when Kristina opened it, she saw that it was a cocktail cabinet from which she produced a bottle of Aquavit, and poured generous measures for all, including Tyra.

'Skål!' smiled their hostess, raising her glass to each of them in turn. 'Good health!'

Helen thought the drink tasted of the aniseed balls she used to buy at the corner shop on her way to school. But she felt warmed and soothed by the alcohol, and the welcome in Kristina's eyes as she toasted her that night.

She thought that she had never seen Peter looking so relaxed.

Until Kristina said, 'Your father will be home on Wednesday.' And a shadow momentarily fell over the happiness in the room.

-0-0-0-

Helen didn't sleep in Peter's room. She wasn't surprised,

as it wouldn't have been allowed at her own parents' house either. But Kristina was apologetic about it. She assumed that the young couple must be sleeping together at college, and explained, as she showed Helen to one of the guest rooms, that Isak would not tolerate them sharing a bed under his roof unless, or until they were married.

Peter, as everyone knew he would, came creeping down the corridor when they were all settled for the night. 'Tyra has a crush on you,' he said, pulling the patchwork quilt up to their ears and snuggling tightly into her. He felt around with his feet for the hot water bottle Kristina had placed at the bottom of the bed to ward off the cold of the ancient bedroom.

Helen laughed at this. 'She's at a girl's school,' she murmured, enjoying the warmth of his body against her back. 'It's practically compulsory. She'll grow out of it when she starts meeting boys.' She had no idea what she was talking about, of course. All her ideas about such things came from books.

-0-0-0-

The next day was Peter's Birthday. At college, he'd complained about being born so close to Christmas. His aunts and uncles always bought him joint Christmas and Birthday presents. But his sister and mother conspired to make it a special day for him, with a late breakfast of coffee and his favourite Filmjölk Loaf, freshly made with hazelnuts and lingonberries and pumpkin seeds on top.

Faced with the dilemma of what to buy for two occasions so close, Helen had agonised over her choices. She didn't want to get something that seemed too intimate. And she couldn't afford anything expensive. In the end, she'd bought a new guitar strap, to wrap and leave under the tree for Christmas. And for his birthday, she'd found a copy of Leonard Cohen's novel, 'Beautiful Losers', in an independent bookshop just off Charing Cross Rd. She hadn't read it, of course. Later, when she did, she realised that it had been a risky book to give to a relatively new boyfriend, in the public glare of the breakfast table, on only the second day of meeting his family. But back then, she'd just thought that Peter loved Leonard Cohen's music, so he was bound to love his books too.

Now, over breakfast, she found her heart beating faster, fired up by strong coffee and anticipation. Kristina had given a cashmere sweater in pale blue that he'd instantly put on, casting his old one over the back of his chair. The colour perfectly complemented his eyes, as his mother had known it would. And he'd thrown his arms around her and whispered, 'Thanks Mum. Love you!' as he kissed her. Tyra had given the newly released debut album by Wishbone Ash. He'd enthused about the concert they'd been to where the band had played support for Deep Purple. And she'd had hugs and kisses too. And now, he was opening her parcel, having accorded her the honour of saving it till last. And all eyes were on her gift as he pulled it from its wrapping. So they all saw his face as it fell.

Helen realised, when she obsessed about it afterwards, what she hadn't noticed before, that Peter only ever really read when he had to. And later, witnessing the dynamic with his father, she understood that the word 'loser' in the title must have been like a knife to his heart. She watched him rally, like the polite young man he was. Saw him force a smile onto his face and kiss her as he had with his mother and sister just moments before.

But she knew she'd chosen something he didn't like. And she felt devastated by that.

Tyra, who was sitting to his right, tried to repair the damage.

'Wow!' she said. 'I've been wanting to read this for ages, but it's been banned all over the place. Can I borrow it when you've read it Pete?'

'Yeah,' Peter had collected himself sufficiently by then to be able to joke with her. 'Provided I get it back. You know what you're like with books.'

Helen glanced at Kristina. She'd had no idea that the book had ever been banned, and she knew that her own mother would have had 'a thing or two to say' about her reading any such thing when she was Tyra's age.

But Kristina was starting to clear the table and seemed not to have noticed the brief rupture in the happiness of the day.

Helen thought then that she was like some kind of Sleeping Beauty, in a trance where only nice things could be seen. It added to her charm, but it was a trait that was already leading to destruction.

-0-0-0-

The day after Peter's Birthday, they decorated the house for Christmas. The Alström traditions were a heady mix of Nordic and British. They went to the village and brought home a massive fir tree to place in the hallway. And then, they put decorations everywhere. Straw goats and gnomes with Santa hats and long beards. Candles and twinkling fairy lights. Strings of tiny Swedish flags around the tree and oak mantelpiece.

And finally, when they'd finished, and eaten a buffet supper, they gathered around the piano for carols.

Helen could still remember how the roaring log fire had made her face tingle with heat. The disappointment of getting the present wrong still tugged at her good mood. But Peter had been upbeat all day. And Tyra had been as irrepressible as ever, keen to chatter on about the decorations and the traditions as if she were saying, 'Don't let it get you down. You weren't to know.'

They were all so spontaneously musical. Peter and Kristina sang carols, while Tyra accompanied them on piano. They both tried to persuade Tyra to sing 'Silent Night', but she was bashful and refused. So, they had home baked gingerbread and several glasses of glögg and played board games in front of the fire instead.

-0-0-0-

Helen knew she'd fallen under the spell of the Alströms. She began to feel sad that Peter would be driving her home to her own family on Christmas Eve. Though she knew that in their own way, they would be missing her and longing to have her home.

But then, Isak Alström returned.

She disliked him instantly. Hated the way his eyes hovered over her body when Peter introduced him to her. She thought he looked at her like a farmer eyeing a cow at market. She hated the transformation in Kristina too. Peter's naturally vibrant and spontaneous mother became pre-emptively edgy and nervous on the morning of her husband's return; checking and double checking that everything was tidy, and that they had all his favourite food and drinks in the house.

It puzzled Helen that this otherwise glowing and confident woman should be so fearful of her husband.

But she understood when she'd met him.

Peter had become increasingly jittery as the time of his father's arrival drew closer too.

And, on the morning of her father's return, Tyra announced suddenly that she was going into London by train to meet one of her school friends for some last minute Christmas shopping on Oxford Street.

Her mother was edgy about this.

'You will be back by six, won't you?' she asked, for the third time over breakfast that morning.

Tyra was piling butter and thick Seville marmalade onto a slice of brown toast. She licked her fingers. 'I told you Mum. I will. I promise!'

'Because that's when your dad will be getting home.'

'Yes, I know. You told me!'

But, of course, she wasn't home by six. She wasn't even home by half past, when her father, held up by Christmas traffic, turned in at the gates of Renton Hall.

Thinking about it now, Helen wondered if Tyra deliberately pushed her luck with him in an effort to be treated like the rest of the family. But, back then, she was still his Golden Girl, and it seemed she could do no wrong.

At 6.32pm, finally alerted by the sound of car tyres on the gravel driveway, Kristina ushered the two young lovers outside to greet the Master of the House. Their three faces were shadowy as they formed a line, haloed by the light pouring through the hallway and out of the front door. Kristina and Peter were both agitated by Tyra's continuing absence. And Isak climbed from his vintage Bentley with a face like thunder. 'Shut the bloody door!' he roared, 'You're letting all the heat escape. And where's my girl, damn it? Keeping warm inside… if she's got any sense!'

Isak was in a foul mood. His books were caught in the beginning of their 1970's hiatus. It would be twelve more years before macho films like Rambo fired the public imagination and brought film moguls to his door seeing the potential for Hollywood profit in his all action heroes. Reviewers were openly describing him as a 'has-been'. And Peter whispered to Helen afterwards, as if fearful that his all-mighty father might hear and punish him, that the hard-to-buy-for husbands were getting different gifts that year. Hai Karate aftershave, and books by more fashionable authors such as Kurt Vonnegut and Mario Puzo.

Tyra finally rolled in at 7pm and just in time to wash and change for dinner at 7.30. She'd missed her train, she said as she took her seat at the table under her father's fond gaze. 'Enjoying the bright lights eh?' he asked benignly. 'Chip off the old block.'

This segued neatly into his favourite topics; himself; the idiot bookshop owners; his pernicious publisher; and the corruptible reviewers who were undoubtedly being bribed by his rivals.

'There's no honour in this world anymore!' he complained, petulantly, as he carved the beef Kristina had lovingly cooked for him.

Helen, thinking that the meat looked worryingly underdone, wondered if he'd given his wife any attention whatsoever since he'd arrived home.

Certainly, he hadn't said anything to Peter, who was busying himself helping everyone to mashed potato and red cabbage from two large hot dishes in the centre of the table.

Having finished the carving and helped himself to several bloody slices of beef, Isak passed the plate with the rest of the meat to Tyra to hand round and poured himself a fourth glass of wine.

Then he waved the bottle in Helen's direction.

'So?' he demanded, suddenly, like a performer inviting a member of the audience to join him on stage. 'Helen....' He seemed proud of himself for remembering her name. 'What do you think about Peter's hair? Makes him look like a girl, don't you think? Reckon we should have called him Petra.... Damned relieved he's got a girlfriend at last, to be honest. I was starting to think he was a Nancy boy!'

Helen tried to brush these comments away, along with the proffered wine, telling Isak shyly that she loved Peter's hair, that it was fashionable and made him look like a rock star.

His father snorted with laughter. 'Bloody rock stars!' he scoffed. 'Pack of prancing pansies, the whole damn lot of 'em. We're too soft with lads nowadays. Should bring back National Service. That'd give 'em all a bit more backbone.'

'Isak!!! I'm sure Helen likes everything about Peter,' said his wife, softly, trying to rescue both Helen and her son.

Helen noticed that she had used the English pronunciation of both her children's names since their father's return. And on later visits she realised that this was always the case. When Isak was in residence the whole household followed his rules.

Darkness flashed into his eyes. His brow furrowed. And his fist clenched.

'Then she's a bloody fool!' he snapped.

Kristina seemed shocked by this rudeness to a guest. She sank back into her chair, half raising her hand in a gesture of conciliation. Sharp red blotches of embarrassment rose to her cheeks, visible, even through her carefully applied make-up.

Opposite Helen, Tyra glanced anxiously at her parents.

'Could I have another glass of wine please Dad?' she asked, by way of deflection.

Her father's expression softened instantly. 'Of course you can my darling!' he said, reaching over to pour the girl her second glass of rich red Bordeaux from the bottle he was still clutching in his ham-like fist. He winked conspiratorially at her. 'Give you another couple of years and you'll be able to drink that milk-sop brother of yours under the table.'

-0-0-0-

Lying now, on the bed in the guest room, Helen thought how prophetic those words had been. And how both of Tyra's parents in their own ways had laid the seeds of her addiction to alcohol.

But, of course, in Isak, there were other addictions too…

That night after the strain of the meal, the young people

made their excuses early and headed for their rooms. Peter kissed Helen by her door. 'I won't come tonight,' he whispered. 'I don't want to risk Dad finding out and kicking off.'

Helen had felt half disappointed and half relieved. The evening had unsettled her. And much as she would have liked the comfort of Peter's warmth beside her, she felt a little scared of Isak Alström too, and keen to avoid his wrath.

She'd tossed and turned for a long time in the dark, unable to sleep.

When her door latch clicked, and the door creaked ajar, she'd felt pleased at first, thinking that Peter had changed his mind, and come to hold her through the night.

But the shadowy figure remained in the doorway. Still. Watching her.

A cold chill ran down her spine. She held her breath, and felt her eyes begin to water as she strained to see through the near darkness of the room. She wondered if this was how a mouse felt when the shadow of a cat fell upon it.

And then she heard Tyra's urgent voice saying, 'Dad!' And the shadow stepped back and closed the door.

-0-0-0-

The next day, as Peter was putting Helen's suitcase in the boot of his Ford Capri, Kristina and Tyra came out to say goodbye.

Isak, apparently, was engrossed in writing in his study. Helen was glad.

'It's been lovely meeting you at last,' said Kristina. 'Peter has told me so much about you. Please don't be put off by

Isak's ill temper last night. He was just disappointed by the tour, and very tired.'

Helen caught the scent of Kristina's hair, and felt the warmth and softness of her body as she held her. 'Thank you so much,' she said. 'You've been incredibly kind to me.'

She turned to Tyra next, thinking how easily she'd fallen into the spontaneous hugging of the Alströms. But the girl had seemed subdued that morning, and now she was holding back a little, as if she were unsure how to say goodbye. Helen felt the shadows of the night before hanging over them. She bundled the kid into her arms and felt her melting there. It was surprisingly comforting to hold her. 'Thank you for making me so welcome,' she whispered. And then, when she was sure Kristina was busy exhorting Peter to drive carefully. 'I had the strangest dream last night. I dreamt there was someone coming into my room and you saved me from them.'

Tyra gave a small uncomfortable laugh and broke away from her. 'You probably saw one of our resident ghosts,' she said. 'Didn't Peter warn you? The place is full of them.'

Nine

When Peter phoned with the funeral details, Tyra wondered if the decent thing would be to attend. But she knew that she couldn't.

'I hope it goes okay,' she said.

'I suppose that means you won't come?' said her brother, flatly.

'I guess so!'

'Okay. Well, take care then.'

'You too!'

Tyra hung up first. With the conversation she'd been dreading over, she hoped she could safely forget about England again for a while.

But, of course, she couldn't do that either. There were too many secrets. And too many lies.

And then there was Helen....

In 1970, when Peter had shyly told her he'd 'met someone', she'd expected somebody pretty and a bit dim, like his only other two girlfriends, Pet (short for Petunia) and Celine. They'd been 'bussed in' from the girls' 'Finishing Establishment' down the road to provide dance partners and possible wives for the future MPs, Surgeons, Barristers and Captains of Industry at his boarding school. And they'd very quickly realised that Peter was never going to be any of the above and moved on.

But Helen wasn't like the Finishing School girls. She was pretty, and kind of sexy, in her short plaid miniskirt and white acrylic sweater and knee length boots. Her hair was a shiny brunette with bronze highlights. And it tumbled over her shoulders in waves that looked completely natural. Her voice was soft and low, with the strangest of Northern accents, like something from Coronation Street, but not quite. And her deep hazel eyes were full of such a longing to be accepted, that Tyra wanted to hug her till she forgot that she had ever felt insecure.

She'd liked this new girlfriend of her brother's instantly. Felt drawn by her kindness and her intelligence. She felt protective of the way she wasn't entirely sure which knife and fork to use at dinner. And, in her youthful naiveté, had imagined that she simply felt grateful that Helen so clearly loved Peter, who could be a bit of a dick sometimes out of his own insecurities.

It took her a long time to realise what Peter had seen right from the start. That she 'liked' Helen in other ways too. Back then, she'd thought that women didn't like other women that way unless they looked like Radclyffe Hall, or her gym teacher, Miss Britten, who had 'favourites' and lurked around the changing rooms in inappropriate ways.

Tyra was glad she'd never attracted the dubious attentions of Miss Britten.

It was hard enough coping with her dad.

She dreaded the nights when she'd be startled from her sleep to find him standing, staring at her, glassy eyed, like some horror movie vampire. The first time it happened, in the Easter holidays after her twelfth birthday, she'd screamed out in terror, and he'd hushed her, telling her that he'd suffered trauma as a deck boy in the wartime merchant navy convoys too terrible to speak of, or imagine. He told her that sometimes, when the stress became too great for him, he would roam the house in his sleep checking on his loved ones. 'Please don't tell your mother,' he'd said. 'I don't want her to worry about me.'

She knew the truth now, of course. It sickened her, just as much as it had when she'd first discovered it.

But she'd believed his story all those years. Even in the nights she'd turned over to find him lying beside her. One night, she'd tried pulling her chest of drawers across so that the door wouldn't open. But the sound of his scratching and rattling at the door was so eerie, she'd never done it again.

And then she'd found him in Helen's doorway, and seen the truth of the matter.

She'd wondered about telling her mother. Kristina often joked about waking to find Isak gone from her side in bed. She seemed to believe that when he disappeared, he must be burning the midnight oil, writing, in his study.

Tyra had tried, so many times, to find a way to tell her the truth. But when it came to it, she always found that she couldn't destroy her mother's happiness like that.

So she'd kept his secret.

It was one of her many regrets.

Ten

27TH MARCH 2019

The afternoon of Isak's funeral was mild with patchy sunshine and a light breeze bobbing the heads of the daffodils that lined the verges. Elin felt uncomfortable, squeezed into the first limousine with her family. She was sandwiched between Dave and two of her grandfather's sisters who had travelled from Sweden for the occasion. Her father and Lucy sat opposite, next to Fred and Brooke. The great grandchildren had been deemed too young for funerals and left in the care of their maternal grandparents in America. The traditional white ties of her father and brother provided the only light relief in a sea of black and blue. Her father's face was grey and set, as if carved from marble. Like the monument he would no doubt commission for the tiny patch of churchyard where his father's ashes would be scattered later, on some unspecified date in a private family ceremony.

No one spoke. Fred fiddled with his collar, which was too tight. He wasn't used to wearing a suit and tie, and he looked all wrong in it. Brooke was accustomed to guiding him through difficult social situations. She put her hand gently on his and held it firmly on the grey leather seat to stop him fidgeting.

Elin felt sad that her mother wasn't in the car with them. She knew Fred would have liked her there. And she was sure her father would have preferred her quiet presence to that of Lucy, who persisted in dribbling tears as if she'd miraculously had a closer relationship with her grandfather than either of her two siblings. But Helen had said firmly that she would come in her own car, directly from home. Elin couldn't say she blamed her.

The villagers had turned out in force to bid goodbye to their oldest celebrity. Isak had been good to them, donating signed first editions of his novels for raffle prizes, obliging with witty talks to the Women's Institute when asked, and employing a good few generations of local people in the house and grounds over the years. They weren't to know that he'd always referred to them privately as the 'peasants'. And they lined the streets now, with heads bowed in deference, as the hearse and cortege were led through the town.

Elin kept her head down too, glancing covertly from time to time at her father. She was worried about him. And she hated to see Lucy clucking over him like a jealous wife.

-0-0-0-

The church choir launched into Allegri's 'Miserere' as the funeral procession entered. The coffin wobbled slightly on the uneven shoulders of the men of the family, all unaccustomed to heavy lifting. And Elin, trailing behind, after her great aunts and Lucy, spotted her mother in the second row of the packed church. She thought she looked small and lonely, tucked as far into the shadows as she could be, dwarfed by a stained glass window of the Raising of Lazarus.

The mourners forked as they came to the front of the church; the men clumsily depositing Isak's coffin on the catafalque, while the followers dispersed to the front pews. Elin caught Dave's hand and drew him to the furthest corner in front of her mum, who leaned forward and put her hand gently on her shoulder.

-0-0-0-

In Spain, Tyra gazed out across the mountains. She'd spent her morning in meditation. Then during the free time of the afternoon, she'd hiked along the old Moorish mule trail that started at the edge of the retreat centre and zigzagged up around the mountainside. She'd walked briskly, focussing on the path and the scuff of her boots against the rocks and grit. Sometimes, when she stopped for long enough, she could hear the whisper of wind fingering through the scrubby broom bushes that were just coming into bud. She'd noticed only the most stunning things along the way. The wild herbs, orchids, and a goshawk riding the currents of cool mountain air.

When she arrived back at the centre, the sun was low. The black silhouettes of the prayer flags fluttered like a flock of starlings against a fuchsia and orange sky. Her calves ached with the exertion of the walk. But the rest was like a dream. She looked at her watch.

In England now, the funeral and committal for cremation

would be over. At the Old Rose Inn in the village, people would be drinking, reminiscing, celebrating the life of a man they'd never really known.

The mountain breeze felt cool against Tyra's cheeks. She breathed it deeply into her lungs. She wanted to feel happy that Isak Alström was gone.

But she just felt bereft.

Eleven

While the family accompanied Isak on his final journey to the Crematorium, Helen had been entrusted with making sure everyone was comfortably settled at the 'Old Rose'. Her head had been throbbing for days, and with a substantial amount of cash behind the bar, she was starting to be concerned that it wasn't the only thing getting hammered. She glanced surreptitiously at her watch. She'd always felt shy and a little out of her depth in large drunken gatherings. And she hoped the more socially adept members of the family would come soon and share the load with her.

She'd heard whispered speculation that she and Peter may be trying to 'make another go of it' too. She prayed that he didn't have any hopes in that direction.

But she felt relieved when she saw him shuffling dejectedly across the car park, arm linked by a protective Lucy, and with Elin and Fred and their partners straggling at a safe distance behind.

Finally, she could relax a little, and maybe, even think of getting ready to go home.

She enveloped Fred and Brooke in comforting hugs and

kisses and enquiries after the grandchildren while Elin busied herself with getting drinks at the bar. She made a good team with Dave, who handed them round to the family, before rolling his tie into his pocket and wandering off with his own pint to inspect the buffet.

'Here Mum, get this down you!' Elin said finally, when her brother and his wife had wandered off to be polite to other people. She handed Helen a glass of Coke. 'You look wiped out, so I got you the real thing. Sugar and caffeine. You look like you need it.'

Helen took the drink gratefully. She'd had a coffee when she got to the pub and been so busy keeping everyone else happy since, it hadn't occurred to her to get herself another drink.

'Thank you sweetheart. I certainly do!'

She took a long, grateful gulp. 'If I weren't driving, I think I'd be hitting the strong stuff today,' she admitted, looking enviously at Elin's large glass of Prosecco. 'Did Dave draw the short straw?'

Elin laughed. 'God, no! I wouldn't inflict that on him. We're getting a taxi. I reckon we're in for the long haul now. We've put Dido in the kennels. You should have seen her little face as we left her! I am so going to be in the doghouse when I collect her tomorrow. But anyway, Mum… how are you bearing up? It can't have been easy sitting through all that…. I mean… Beautiful music! I loved the Tallis at the end. But all the hellfire and brimstone from the vicar…. Blimey, what was he on?'

Helen laughed at Elin's vehemence. She'd always felt

passionately about things. It was one of the many things she loved about her.

'I'm fine,' she said. 'And the vicar did get a bit carried away I must admit.'

'You're not kidding... All that 'Day of Judgement' stuff? I thought some avenging angel was going to come crashing through the window behind the altar at any minute!'

Her voice raised as she warmed to the subject. Her mum looked anxious.

'Watch out sweetheart, he's here... somewhere!' Helen swept the room looking for him, and eventually located him amongst Peter's cluster of commiserants. 'Oh, it's ok, he's boring your dad.' She relaxed, visibly. She'd already suffered the vicar's opinions about what a 'True Christian' Isak had been. It seemed to be a common view among people who didn't really know him.

-0-0-0-

By 9pm the gathering in The Old Rose had descended into merriment. And the chatter volume was rising, as people vied to tell amusing anecdotes about the deceased.

Helen had made her excuses and gone home long since. She planned to banish thoughts of her father-in-law with several glasses of Bailey's, and a few episodes of 'Orange is The New Black'.

Elin and Dave were slowly weaving their way through the throng, saying their goodbyes.

Fred and Brooke were feeling 'out of it' in a corner by the door.

And across the rowdy room, Max, Peter's old drummer, spotted his bandmate coming out of the Gents, where he'd gone to escape Lucy, and took the opportunity to pounce.

'Sorry about your dad mate,' he said, tapping Peter on the shoulder and almost making him jump out of his skin. 'Wow, those nerves of yours are bad!' he added, feeling mildly guilty for startling someone so recently bereaved.

Peter looked flustered. 'You nearly had me joining him then,' he said.

Max could see that Peter wasn't happy to see him, but he had no intention of allowing that to dent his resolve. 'He had a good innings though, right?'

'If I'd a pound for everyone who's said that today, I'd be rich.'

Max laughed. 'You Alströms have always been loaded anyway!' he shot back. 'Hey, that vicar was a right grim old bugger though, wasn't he? You should've had it at my place. I'd have had 'em rocking the aisles.'

'That's why I didn't ask you,' said Peter, glancing around quickly, as Helen had done earlier, to make sure the vicar wasn't within earshot. 'And he's a family friend.'

'I'm glad I never came to any dinner parties at your house then! Danny sends his love BTW.'

'He couldn't manage to get here though?'

'Well, he probably could. But you know funerals aren't his thing.... Anyway, now you've got today over with, how about you get back to the band? It'll cheer you up. Give you something to take your mind off all the doom and gloom.'

'Ok.' Peter seemed skittish and evasive. He pointed towards

Elin who was waving to him from the door. 'I'd better just say goodbye to the kids.'

'Sure man. No probs. Next practice is Monday afternoon, 2 o'clock. At my church hall as usual. We need to get some serious time in you know. Easter will be a write-off for me, and the gig's only five weeks away now.'

'Yeah, sure. Text the details through to me. And thanks for coming. I appreciate it.'

Max didn't think he did. He had a bet on with Danny that Peter was bailing out on Alstrom.

That's me ten quid richer he thought as he watched his old bandmate weaving his way through the crowd.

-0-0-0-

In Spain, the stars were out. Tyra stood in the doorway of her cabin and gazed up at the glittering night sky. She felt the ancient rock beneath her feet and the infinite galaxies above. She was grateful for her insignificance in the vastness of it all. Here in her small world, she smelt wood smoke on the cold night air. And she remembered her much younger self burning everything that reminded her of her father. She thought of Helen. And her mother. And Peter. All lost over the years. She went inside, sat down at the desk with her Buddha and candle, and began to write…

Night falls, and I hear you calling. Day breaks my heart. Stars cast their light across the universe and die before we see them. And all is lost, suddenly, shattering my soul...

Twelve

Peter knew, deep down, that he'd driven Helen away. And not just tonight, when she had been visibly relieved to get away from the funeral gathering. He knew that he'd quickly become a disappointment to her in their life together too. It wasn't surprising. He'd always believed that she'd see him eventually as he saw himself, a pathetic loser who wasn't very much of a man at all.

He felt clueless with his children without her. So, he'd been relieved to retreat to his bedroom when he got back to the house at just before midnight with Lucy, Fred, and Brooke in tow.

It felt easier than sitting around trying to talk to them without Helen's help.

He'd always felt clumsy and inadequate with Fred. And he struggled to know what to say to Brooke, whose quick-fire delivery, combined with his own insidiously creeping deafness, often made her sentences unintelligible to him.

And Lucy, who was going to be staying till Sunday, was driving him mad. If anyone was the true heir to Isak, it was Peter's eldest daughter. Moderately successful, but never satisfied, in her job as a conference organiser in Sweden, she'd always been a 'glass half empty' kind of a girl. It had been quite endearing in her youth. Something the family could tease her about, chorusing 'Glass half full Luce, glass half full.' But anyone who dared to tease her now would do so at their peril. Over the years, there had been several failed romances with men who'd found her initially attractive and then unbearable to live with. She'd been overlooked for promotion by bosses who despaired of her ever developing any people skills. And, without the will to examine her own part in any of her failures, she had become a sour and judgmental workaholic.

The only saving grace, from Peter's perspective, had always been that he could do no wrong in Lucy's eyes. For reasons known only to her, she'd chosen to hero-worship him from day one. He supposed that must be better than being on the receiving end of her contempt, as Helen and Fred and Elin so frequently were. But it was wearing thin now, especially as she seemed to have got the idea that he should come and live with her in a 'grandad flat' in Sweden, so she could 'keep an eye on him'. The thought made him feel queasy. And he was starting to understand how suffocated Tyra must have felt, squirming in the toxic glow of their father's favour.

All in all, even with a heavy dose of diazepam, the day had felt too much for him. And now it seemed as if it all must have happened to someone else. An actor, maybe, playing a grieving son in a film. At least he could comfort himself that the soundtrack had been good.

But it was cold comfort in the grand scheme of things.

Peter thought that maybe, if he'd been alone, he might have put the TV on and slept on the sofa.

He found it hard to sleep in the bed he had shared for so many years with Helen. It felt too lonely. But even so, it was better than having to cope with his children.

He couldn't cry anymore either. When Helen had left, he'd cried for days as if a great dam had breached its walls and destroyed every living thing around him. He'd turned to the familiar numbing comfort of tranquillizers and antidepressants to stem the flow. He knew from other times that the tablets would keep the tears inside where no-one else could see. There'd been things to do. People to tell. And their responses to cope with. Not least his father, who he'd left till last, and who had taken the opportunity to mock him for his inadequacy, just as he had always done.

The image of the dead Isak haunted him. He saw him everywhere. In his dreams, of course. But also, in the mirror when he was shaving. And today in the side aisle of the church, hovering close to Helen, and later in the driveway of the crematorium, biding his time, invisible to everyone but the son he'd always despised.

Peter had told himself that once the funeral was over, that whole chapter would be finished.

But now he wondered if he'd ever be free of it.

In an effort at distraction, he picked up his phone from the bedside table and started to browse through the newsfeed, stopping from time to time to read more about the political infighting over Brexit; complaints about planning for new homes locally; and then a headline that made his blood run cold.

A Village Farewell
Isak Alström 1924-2019

Today, the villagers of Little Stockham bade an emotional farewell to Isak Alström, their most illustrious adopted son.

Born in the Swedish seaside town of Mölle in 1924, the young Isak followed his brother into the merchant navy as a deck boy just as war broke out in Europe. A committed Anglophile, and critical of the neutral stance taken by his home country, Isak was proud to have sailed in merchant shipping convoys for the Allies. His first novel, **Hell Storm**, was inspired by his youthful experience of the horror and heroism of those times. The book is dedicated to the 1,500 Swedish men and women who perished in the convoys, a number that sadly, included Isak's own brother Lars.

In happier times, **Hell Storm** brought love, as well as literary fame for Isak. At the book's launch, he met popular jazz singer Kristina Berg, youngest daughter of hotelier Mikel Berg. Spotting the blonde beauty across the crowded room, a smitten Isak climbed onto a table, grabbed a glass of champagne, and called a toast... 'To the angel who has stolen my heart.'

The couple married later that year, and were blessed with two children, Peter, and Tyra.

Isak's books achieved worldwide success, translated into 22 languages, and climbing bestseller lists from Reykjavik to Wellington. But his biggest sales were always here in the UK. So, it was no surprise when, in 1963, the family bought Renton Hall, close to the village of Little Stockham, and permanently settled there.

Isak often described the decade that followed as the happiest of *his life. With his beloved Kristina at his side, he was a regular supporter of charitable events in the area. His books enjoyed enduring popularity, and their children Peter and Tyra seemed set to follow in their mother's musical footsteps, as founders of the rock band 'Alstrom'.*

But then, in the early hours of August 10th, 1975, tragedy struck. Driving home with Isak after a dinner party with friends, Kristina lost control of her Alfa Romeo in a country lane close to home and crashed into a ditch. A distraught Isak, unable to revive his beloved wife, and despite his own injuries, ran to the nearest house for help, but Kristina had already passed away by the time the emergency services arrived.

Isak never remarried, and often claimed that he had poured his grief into his, increasingly literary, later novels.

Struggling to come to terms with the loss of her mother, Tyra spiralled into drug and alcohol abuse, and now lives in Europe.

Alstrom are enjoying an unexpected revival this year. Their song 'You Watching Me', is the theme tune for the Scandinavian Thriller 'The Fördömelse Code'. Isak, in a rare recent interview, joked that his son, Peter, was reforming the band, and expressed the hope that he would not ask to practice in the coach house as he had when he was a teenager.

Possibly Peter was going to ask his dad just that when he called round to see him at 7.30pm on the 20th of February. But sadly, he found that his much loved father had died of a stroke earlier that evening.

Today's funeral was held at St Mark's Church, Little Stockham, and conducted by the Rev William H. Battersby. The family attended a private committal at Parndon Wood Crematorium afterwards. Refreshments were provided at The Old Rose Inn, in the village.

The mourners were led by Isak's son Peter, and grandchildren Lucy, Frederik, and Elin.

Isak's daughter Tyra was not in attendance.

Peter stared for a long time at the screen. He recognised his father's perennial themes. Heroism, romantic love, proud parenthood, and tragic loss. Isak had told these tales about himself so many times that he probably even believed them. The old man was a gifted storyteller, after all.

But Peter had lived with him, and he remembered the misery of being banished to the old coach house with his violin when his father was home. Isak never could endure 'that screeching of mating cats'. He remembered the cobwebs and the spiders lurking in the far corners, the half-light from the single bulb, and the vintage Bentley nestling under its ghostly dust cover. He'd thought that Tyra was lucky then, being allowed to practice piano in the cosiness of the sitting room. But he sensed now that she had endured a different kind of torment in the spotlight of their father's hungry gaze. He wondered, with the greater empathy of age, if that gaze had fed her all-consuming terror of being centre stage.

And, as to the rest... Peter had spoken to his grandparents and uncles. Small secrets had been let slip in unguarded moments, and he'd pieced together the truth about his father and the war.

He'd seen too, with his own eyes, Isak's controlling behaviour towards the 'angel who stole his heart'. Kristina had learnt to placate her husband or suffer the consequences. If she ever dared be anything other than an ornament to Isak in public, she would be accused of flirting, or boring people with 'her nonsense'. As teenagers in the backseat of the car, Peter and Tyra had often felt their father's thwarted narcissism in his angry silences and sulks and snide remarks. And they knew, but always denied to themselves, how cold and cruel his fury could be behind closed doors.

The dinner party on the night she died had, by all accounts, been convivial. And Peter had long suspected that Isak, too drunk to drive, and unconstrained by the presence of witnesses, would have been punishing his wife in some way as she attempted to navigate the winding country lanes in the dark.

But he'd never had anything concrete until now.

Any illusions Peter may have had about Isak Alström had been destroyed, one by one in the grim reality of life at Renton Hall. But still, until their final showdown, he had never given up hope that someday he might do something big enough to make the old man love him. He knew now that Isak had been incapable of love. And when he thought of that, despite the antidepressants, tears of grief welled in his eyes.

Thirteen

The next morning Helen read the same piece. She'd collapsed, almost literally, into bed as soon as she got home the previous night, all thoughts of Bailey's or box set abandoned to the pounding in her head. And she woke amidst shadowy dream-ghosts that fled the moment she turned on her bedside lamp.

The funeral had been a strain. Despite years of pretending that all was well around her father-in-law, the masquerade had never been easy. During Isak's lifetime, she had always sensed that he took her silence as vindication. That she had somehow taken his shame into herself, and by saying nothing, had proclaimed herself guilty.

She'd wondered if there would be some grim satisfaction in seeing his coffin carried into church. But she'd found she couldn't believe he was in there. She felt that his spectre still lived beside her, whispering that he would never be truly dead, until all those whose lives he wrecked had also breathed their last.

It was a bleak thought. And the morning seemed to match it. When she forced herself to get up and open the curtains, she saw grey sky and rooftops still wet with rain. And she felt daunted that the long idleness of a retirement day would be broken only by the distraction of lunch with Fred and Brooke, and the sadness of waving them goodbye as they set off for their long flight home.

She told herself that she, at least, was happy here, in her own space. The flat was cosy and easy to manage. She liked the bland walls and sage carpets. She loved her balcony with just a couple of chairs and manageable tubs of daffodils with tulips waiting in bud. And she felt grateful that, after years of feeling responsible for a family home, she now had a landlord to fix things when they went wrong.

She shrugged into her dressing gown and went to the kitchen to make strong coffee, then huddled with her phone, flicking through the messages from friends who knew some of the truth.

Her old friend Bridget had been first off the mark…

Hey sweets, how did it all go? Fancy a chat later?

And a couple of others had come after that…

Hope you gave the old bastard a good send-off!

Been thinking of you. Give us a ring when you're up to it.

She didn't feel up to it. Not yet. Though the thought of people there for her was comforting.

The coffee felt harsh on her stomach. She wondered if she should eat. But she didn't want to.

For lack of energy to do anything different, she flicked to the newsfeed on her phone, as Peter had done the night before.

The article about Isak, or maybe just the coffee after all, made her queasy.

She'd seen the authorised version of her father-in-law's life many times before. It had left her with a deep distrust of anything, glowing or otherwise, that she ever read about anyone. She was glad to see that she had not been listed amongst the family mourners. Though, unlike Tyra, she hadn't had the courage to completely stay away.

And seeing Kristina's death raked up again, re-awakened the guilt that lay heavy on her heart.

-0-0-0-

On Monday afternoon, she called round to see how Peter was doing.

To her relief, he seemed a little better, shakily pottering around in the front garden, deadheading daffodils. He was on a 'new generation' antidepressant now. An 'SNRI'. It seemed to be lifting his mood. He looked pleased to see her. And offered his cheek for a kiss.

'Put the kettle on, will you love?' he said. 'I'll be with you in a mo.'

'Ok!'

The phone rang just as she was filling the kettle.

She answered it out of long engrained habit. And then she thought she shouldn't have. She'd spent too much of her life already being Peter's unofficial P.A.

'Hey... Baby!'

It was Max. She always thought he sounded like a higher-pitched version of Barry White. And she'd often wondered how he'd been considered suitable for church ministry. With his tight jeans, and roving eye for 'the ladies', he was an ecclesiastical scandal waiting to happen. All she could think was that he must be a big 'draw' at the annual Greenbelt Festival.

'Hey, Max!' She deliberately injected a note of weariness into her voice, hoping he'd take the hint and get off the line.

But Max didn't take hints. 'You sound stressed!' he said. 'Shall I come round and give you a back rub?'

'Oh, grow up Max! What do you want?'

Max laughed. 'I love grumpy women?' he said.

Helen sighed. 'You have that effect on most of us, do you? And... please don't answer that... Just cut to the chase... What do you want?'

'Ok... don't get your knickers in a knot... How's Pete doing?'

'Ok, I think. Why?'

He didn't answer this immediately. 'Are you two getting back together again then?'

'No.'

'That's a shame... It's hard being alone at our time of life.'

'Mm, I guess.' Helen wasn't finding it hard at all.

'If ever you should get lonely, you know where I am.'

Helen hesitated, wondering whether he was trying to be empathic.

He wasn't, of course. She realised that as he pushed on, encouraged by her silence.

'I mean, you've always been out of bounds... Mate's bird, and all that... But I've always fancied you.'

'You fancy any woman with a pulse Max.'

'That's a 'no' then, is it?'

'It's a never in a million years.'

'Well, that's a bit harsh.'

She laughed, ground down by his incorrigibility.

'Look, you idiot…. Just cut to the chase will you? What do you want? Can I take a message?'

'You could congratulate the idle bugger on missing yet another rehearsal if you want!'

Helen cursed under her breath. She fell into default making-excuses-for-Peter mode. 'It must have slipped his mind.'

Max scoffed. 'Slipped down his list of priorities, more like. I keep telling him, he's no use to us if he can't be bothered. The gig's just round the corner now and we're going to make total dicks of ourselves if we're not careful.'

Helen found herself lowering her voice. 'Maybe you should postpone,' she whispered. 'All this stuff with his dad has come as a real shock to him. I don't think he's going to be able to concentrate on a 'come-back' any time soon.'

Max tutted knowingly. 'I bet he's gone into one of his depressions, hasn't he? I thought he was looking a bit peaky at the funeral.'

'Well, possibly… Though I don't think you can technically call it depression if someone's just been bereaved.'

'No, but since the miserable bugger's been in the doldrums for most of his life…'

Helen couldn't dispute this.

'Danny'll be gutted if we call it a day now.'

'I'm sure you both will!'

'No sign of Tyra then?'

Helen felt herself stiffen, as she always did, when she heard Tyra's name. Over the years it had led to her not wanting to discuss the topic at all. And Peter, sensing this and guessing, rightly, or wrongly, the cause of it, had been all too happy to comply.

'No! I think Peter spoke to her. She's living at some Buddhist monastery in Spain apparently. But I doubt that she'd want to come back.'

'Shame! She was a bloody good singer! And very popular with the ladies. But… about the band. Dan and me… If Pete's not up to it, we're thinking of bringing some session people in. I think we've got as much right to call ourselves 'Alstrom' as him and Tyra ever had.'

'Don't be daft Max! It's their family name, give or take a couple of dots.'

'Well, we stuck with them through thick and thin. And, what with Pete's moods and Tyra's…shall we say… issues… Let's face it, that band would never have got off the starting block if we hadn't been holding it together.'

He had a point. Though Helen wasn't going to encourage him by admitting it.

'Have you got any more rehearsals planned?' she asked.

'11am Friday. At the church hall again. He'll need to be on time. The Over Sixties Art Club's in at 3pm. And I've got to go and do a pre-marriage counselling session in the vestry at half past.'

'*You* doing pre-marriage counselling? Isn't that kind of weird?'

'I know! It's a dirty job, but someone's got to do it.'

'Right!' said Helen. 'Friday. 11 o'clock. I'll do my best to get him there. And seriously Max, please promise me you won't do anything hasty before then. If you and Danny steal his band, in his current frame of mind, I really don't trust him not to do something stupid.'

-0-0-0-

Peter looked weary as he came into the kitchen. Helen forced herself not to say anything as he washed his hands in the kitchen sink and dried them on the tea towel. She knew his gesture was territorial. My house... my rules. If he'd been a dog, he'd have been peeing up the kitchen units to make his point.

'Who were you talking to?' he asked.

Helen handed him a mug of tea. 'It was Max. He's been trying to ring you. You should have been at band rehearsal. But there's another one on Friday at 11am. I said I'd tell you.'

'Ok.'

'Do you think you'll feel up to going?'

'I don't know. I'll text him later.'

'I think I should warn you. They're considering dumping you.'

'Well, I suppose they'll be in good company then!'

Helen ignored the invitation to feel bad about herself. She felt like she'd already suffered enough guilt to last a lifetime.

Peter realised quickly that she wasn't going to respond. So, he directed his self-pity towards the new traitors.

'After everything I did for them!' he said.

Helen wished he would stop whining. It wasn't an attractive way to be.

But she realised that he was still talking to her. And that he'd finished with the subject of the band.

'Shall we take our tea through into the conservatory?' he was asking. 'There are some Daim bars in the cupboard. Lucy brought them with her from home.'

-0-0-0-

Elin discovered her father in one of his wounded moods when she called round to see him that evening. She thought he looked older than he had at the funeral, when he'd combed his hair and smartened himself up. Now, with 5 o'clock stubble and in grubby gardening clothes, he looked frail and defeated.

Dido wasn't helping. Elin had brought her round to cheer him up. But the dog seemed more interested in watching the squirrels bounding up and down the trees in the garden.

'How're you doing Dad?' she asked, cautiously, perching on the cane chair next to the recliner where he seemed to have set up home.

'I think I'm about to get kicked out of Alstrom,' he said, despondently.

Elin laughed. She thought he was joking. But, of course, he wasn't.

'But… What? … Why?'

She stood to open the conservatory door for Dido, who was pawing at the glass.

'It's simple enough. I'm not feeling up to rehearsals. And if I can't get there on Friday, Max and Danny are going to ditch me.'

They watched the dog waddling down the garden path to stare up into the trees.

'I imagine they're just bluffing Dad. I mean, they can't dump you. It's your group!'

Peter sighed. 'They're not bluffing. They think this is their last chance at the big time. And if me and Tyra aren't up to it, they're determined to find people who are.'

'Tyra's not on board either then?' She was pretty sure she already knew the answer to that one. But she felt the need to ask it anyway.

'No.'

'Did you even ask her?'

'There was no point. She'd have said no.'

Elin knew there was no point reasoning with her father either. Not when he was in this kind of mood.

'Well, maybe you'll feel more up to it on Friday,' she said, shrugging. 'How about I build your strength up with a Domino's pizza now Lucy isn't here with her beady eye on your cholesterol levels? I bet she's had you on nothing but carrots and kale for days. But I'm here now. And Dave's out at football, and the night's still young.'

-0-0-0-

In Spain, Tyra was growing uncomfortable with the half lotus position. Her eyes blurred as she gazed downwards at the floor of her cabin. She noticed small dust balls wafting across the floor. She smelt warm candle wax and the sap of the wood stacked beside her log burner. She labelled these observations as 'thinking,' and tried to put them to one side. But then a vague ache in her back started to nag at her attention. The ache was followed rapidly by a longing to straighten out her left leg before her calf muscle contracted into cramp. As usual, meditation felt to her like a penance. And at first, when her phone buzzed on the desk beside the Buddha and flickering candle, she thought some strange and hardy insect must be trapped inside the room, along with all her thoughts.

She raised her unfocused eyes and glanced blearily around to see where the noise was coming from. The buzzing stopped. Then, just as she was about to settle back into meditation, it started again.

She struggled creakily to her feet, following the noise, and finally located it in her mobile. She stared at the phone. She wasn't expecting a call, and she wished it would just shut up. But seeing 'Elin' on the screen, against her better judgment, she answered.

'Hello?' Even to herself, she sounded wary, and a bit paranoid.

'Auntie Tyra?'

There it was again, that Auntie...

'Yes.'

'It's Elin.'

'Yes, I know.' Gathering her thoughts, she added, 'How are you?'

She hoped to goodness that the kid wasn't down in the village at the bar again.

'I'm good, thanks. How are you?'

Tyra wished she hadn't entered into pleasantries now. Elin's voice sounded like she could be wind surfing, and it seemed doubtful that the mobile signal would last for long.

'I'm fine, thanks. What do you want?' Oh God, that probably sounded rude…

But Elin seemed up for getting straight to the point too.

'You've got to come home,' she said, bluntly. 'Dad's still dithering about going back to Alstrom. And Max and Danny are threatening to recruit other people and carry on anyway. We need you back here Tyra. I think you're the only one who can stop it all going horribly wrong. And honestly, I know it's a long shot, but if Dad sees that you've come back to the band… it really might give him the lift he needs to come back too.'

-0-0-0-

Tyra bowed to the teacher as she entered her hut. It was a simple one-room dwelling like hers, though, she couldn't help noticing, much chillier.

'Thank you for seeing me,' she said.

'It's something of a surprise that you've come.'

The incumbent Lama was an astute Spanish woman of about fifty. She had kept her Spanish name of Sofia. Her long grey hair was pulled back in a tight bun. Her face was tanned and sun-wrinkled. And her standard maroon and gold robes were augmented by a thick cashmere shawl that was probably her only nod to luxury.

She faced Tyra with brown eyes so dark they were almost black. And gestured for her to sit.

'So,' she said, in perfect English. 'How can I help you?'

Tyra felt her carefully rehearsed words fleeing in terror at the thought of confiding in someone. She'd learnt that expressing feelings could be dangerous. It always made them, somehow, more real.

'I have a difficult decision to make,' she said. 'And I don't know what to do.'

Sofia sat, observing her gravely. She didn't say anything.

Tyra assumed this was an invitation to continue.

'My dad died a few weeks ago,' she said.

'I'm sorry to hear that.'

'I'm not. I've tried hard to view him with compassion. And I can see that he had his own demons. But he was a cruel man. He did a lot of damage to my mum and my brother.'

Opposite her, Lama Sofia nodded almost imperceptibly. She seemed unfazed by Tyra's indifference to her father's death. Though there was something in her look that suggested she didn't entirely believe it. 'You should continue your compassion practice,' she said, predictably. 'And *you*? Did he damage *you*?'

Tyra didn't want to think about this. 'I was his favourite,' she said. 'That had its own challenges.... Anyway, there's a situation at home. My niece wants me to go back. But I don't know.'

'Why did you leave?'

'I was an addict. I messed things up for everyone. Ran

away. Let everybody down. They all have good reason to hate me.'

'As you hate yourself?'

Tyra looked up, startled. She hadn't realised it was that obvious.

'I guess... Yes... When I think about those times.'

'That must be painful.'

It was a statement, not a question.

Tyra nodded. 'It is when I think about it. But I try not to think about it too often.'

'And when you do, there's always the bar in the village.'

Tyra looked for the censure she usually saw in people's faces when they said things like that. It wasn't there in Sofia.

She hung her head, embarrassed. 'Always a bar somewhere... yes.'

'But you've never thought to go home until now?'

Tyra felt her thoughts longing to escape into that spaced out place where she didn't think, didn't feel. It was hard to stop herself from going there. She looked around the dimly lit room for something to latch on to. On the small shrine beside Sofia's bed, before the Buddha, a candle flickered in a red holder. It cast hypnotic shadows on the painted silk thangka of Guru Rinpoche on the wall behind. She pulled her gaze away and looked out of the window instead, across misty mountains to low lying cloud. It was mid-morning of the second day since Elin's call. And still she was no closer to knowing what she ought to do.

'I almost went back about three years after I left. I was living in France and attending meetings of Narcotics Anonymous. I was working through Steps 8 and 9...'

'To make a list of the people you'd harmed… And to make amends, except when doing so would injure them or others?'

'Yes…. I wanted to do that. But I couldn't. I used to be in a band with my brother and three other guys. I messed things up for them just when they were on the verge of getting somewhere. Nothing I did could repair that. But I wrote to my brother. I think he was pleased to hear from me. It was the first time we'd communicated since I left. He had good news. He was married and had just become a father. He sent me a photo of his wife holding their new-born child. I knew then that I couldn't go back.'

'Why not?'

'Because I was in love with his wife.'

Tyra looked again for signs of condemnation in her teacher's face. But Sofia only seemed thoughtful, her head tilted a little as she looked back at Tyra.

'So now? What's changed?'

'The band are reforming. It might help them if I go back.'

'And your brother? And his wife?'

'They're separated.'

'So, now you have the opportunity to make amends?'

'Yes, I think so.'

'And still, you're not sure.'

Tyra thought about this, trying to find the words to express her misgivings.

'No…. I don't know how my brother will feel about me returning to the band. He's ambivalent about the whole thing for some reason. And I know he's still angry with me for messing up first time round. My niece seems to think it will help if I'm there, but I'm not so sure.'

'And your sister-in-law?'

'That's the hardest thing. I still love her. And when I heard about the separation, I felt this crazy surge of hope. But I know I'm deluding myself. She has every reason to despise me. And I don't blame her.'

Sofia held Tyra's gaze.

'You must do the right thing,' she said.

Tyra felt flustered. This wasn't what she needed. It didn't help.

'How can I know what that is?' she asked, desperately.

'Your conscience knows,' said Sofia. 'Follow it.'

Fourteen

FRIDAY 5TH APRIL 2019

Obediently watching the flight attendant as she semaphored her way through the safety procedures at the front of the plane, Tyra wondered if she was the only person in the cabin who had never actually flown before. Certainly, she seemed to be the only one bothering to listen to the talk. And the guy beside her had already fallen asleep.

Avoiding flying until the grand old age of 65 hadn't been a conscious choice. Nothing as moral as trying to reduce her carbon footprint. Though that seemed to Tyra to be quite an urgent thing to do. It was just that with her family and the band, she'd always travelled by car, or van, and ferry. And since she'd moved to mainland Europe, it had suited her to take buses or trains, or even riverboats every time she upped sticks and moved on.

She was already of the opinion that she hadn't missed much. She felt frazzled by the interminable check-in procedures at the airport, and trapped and claustrophobic in the window seat on the plane. The sleeping man next to her was huge and already starting to snore a little. His suit was rumpled, and he had a sweaty sheen to his face. The budget flight seat was too small for him, and his arm was creeping over the armrest into her space a little more with each long whistling exhale.

She glanced at her watch. With almost 3 hours flying ahead of her, she hoped the trolley service would start soon. She figured that, like most things, this flight would be more tolerable with a few miniatures of Courvoisier to help her through it. But with take-off not even started yet, there didn't seem to be much hope of that for a while.

Resignedly, she scrunched herself as close as she could to the side of the plane. Then she put her seat belt on and closed her eyes. Beside her, the man's snores became deeper, with a worrying little sleep apnoeic pause before each juddering in-breath.

She felt edgy and anxious. The plane was crowded. A baby was screaming at the top of its lungs a couple of seats ahead of her. And she wasn't used to being around so many people.

She felt unsettled by this trip too. She wasn't sure it was a good idea. But she'd listened to Sofia. Deep down, she knew that the old Alstrom fans were more likely to return if she was in the band. And she felt she owed that to Max and Danny at least, after wrecking everything for them first time round.

She still wasn't convinced by Elin's hope that Peter would be more likely to come back to Alstrom if she was there. But maybe it was worth a try.

And then there was Helen. If she was lucky, this trip might give her the chance to apologise at least. To try to heal the harm she'd caused.

She knew that she had no right to hope for more than that.

But…. 'One day at a time', she whispered to herself. It was important not to look too far ahead. Years of N.A. meetings had taught her that much. If not entirely how to stay away from alcohol, which had always been her fall-back drug of choice.

Take-off was scary. The rush and feel of being pushed back in her seat, and the pressure in her ears felt unnatural to her. For a moment, she longed for the days when she would have knocked back diazepam or beta blockers to take the edge off her anxiety. But then she remembered the downward spiral of all that, and tried to breathe instead, consciously unclenching her fists, lowering her shoulders, and telling herself that people did this kind of thing all the time. Hurtling through the air in a metal capsule to face home, family, lost loves. In the grand scheme of things, this was nothing. And anyway, if all went well, she could have a drink very soon, and that never failed to take the edge off everything.

There was a soft purr to the plane's engine now. Curiously, she opened her eyes and looked out of the window. The ground below looked far away, the tiny world of people so insignificant from here, up in the sky. And then, in a blur of dazzling white, they were above clouds that looked like snowy mountain peaks. And, lulled by the familiarity of that landscape, the hum of the plane, the soft ripple of voices, and the faint arrhythmia of her neighbour's snoring, she found herself drifting into sleep.

-0-0-0-

She dreamt of Peter. A memory, though with the surreal, time-hopping quality that only dreams can bring. It was a hot summer's day in the garden of her youth. Their parents were on the patio in front of the house. She remembered the table, with its tight green painted wrought iron swirls, and curled legs that were easy to stub your toes on. The chairs had cushions that were kept in the shed, so they didn't get wet overnight. Their mother was young and radiant, and so in love with Isak, their father. She was hanging on his every word, as she always did. They were drinking cocktails with fruit. Pink, maybe Strawberry Daiquiri. Peter was seven or eight years old. Home from school for the summer. And she was playing with him on the long, gently sloping lawn that ran down to the orchard. He'd made a plane from balsa wood. It was his pride and joy. It glided when he tossed it high into the air. He let Tyra try to fly it too, but she never got the hang of it. So, she'd run with him, chasing it, giggling, with the exhilaration of the sun on her skin, and hero-worship of her brother in her heart. Hours of playing, it seemed, time drifting by. Lying in grass that smelt of camomile, watching ladybirds and ants.

Then, as the sun began to dip, and cast a golden glow, their mum called them into the house.

They pretended they hadn't heard, wanting just five more minutes of that bliss…

That maybe slipped into ten.

Then their father's shadow was over them. His voice booming. Peter ripped from her side.

The slap she heard but didn't see. Because she knew it was coming and looked away.

Seeing, instead, Isak's foot crashing down onto the plane, leaving it in balsa-splinters in the grass.

-0-0-0-

When she woke, she discovered that she'd missed the drinks trolley. The flight attendants were parading the aisles collecting rubbish. Her neighbour was awake now, and had feasted well, judging by the pile of plastic cups and wrappers he was shovelling into the waste bag.

Tyra begrudged it. She was hungry. And her mouth was dry.

Fifteen

Fearful of Tyra getting lost in the airport, Elin parked the car, and hovered around the 'Arrivals' gate. She wasn't terribly hopeful as she scanned the small clusters of people arriving from Malaga. She expected her aunt to come half-cut... If she came at all.

But in the event, she confounded expectations. She looked a little disorientated and grumpy, for sure. But she was sober, and most definitely there.

She even looked pleased to see Elin, though that could just have been relief to be off the plane.

The look morphed into alarm as her niece ran towards her and engulfed her in a hug. In the long years of exile, Tyra had given up on being that close to anyone.

'Auntie Tyra, I'm so glad you came…. Is the rest of your luggage on a trolley somewhere?'

They both looked at the weekend-sized canvas holdall that Tyra was clutching like a shield to fend off Elin's embrace.

'No. This is it. I tend to travel light.'

Elin felt anxious at this. 'You *are* planning on staying

though, aren't you?' she asked, hardly daring to hear the answer.

'Well… yes… Till after the gig… If Max and Danny want me. And if your dad doesn't object. Have you told them all that I'm coming?'

'I've texted Dad. And I don't have phone numbers for the other two. Though if Dad's decided to turn up for the rehearsal, he'll have told them. And we can always get you more things while you're here if you need anything. In fact, we're probably about the same size, so I bet I've got stuff you could borrow.'

Tyra looked doubtful about this. And Elin burbled on… 'Anyway, we can cross that bridge when we come to it. Shall we go and surprise the guys at the Church Hall while they're still there?'

Tyra shrugged. 'Can I get a coffee or something first?' she asked. 'I fell asleep on the plane and missed the damned trolley. My mouth feels like the bottom of a budgie's cage.'

-0-0-0-

She seemed in better spirits by the time she'd armed herself with a Flat White and Danish 'To Go'. And she followed Elin meekly enough to the car.

Small talk wasn't her forte though.

'Was it a good flight?'

'It was okay. I don't think I'll do it again.'

'Oh, gosh! They can be a bit dire! You didn't get stuck next to a mouth-breather, did you?'

There was no answer to this, and Elin glanced across to see Tyra taking a long slurp of her coffee.

She decided to focus on driving, following the same arrows that Dave had negotiated when he'd collected her, but considerably faster and without having to vacate the car at the ticket barrier.

'It must seem weird being back in England,' she ventured, when she could see that her aunt had lowered the coffee cup and not yet begun to unwrap the apricot pastry.

'Yes,' said Tyra, gazing out of the window at grimy banks of dying roadside daffodils. 'I'd forgotten how grey it is.'

'Well, it's not always grey.'

'No, I guess not. How was the funeral?'

'A bit bleak. Dad chose nice music. But the vicar was totally up himself, chuntering on about the Resurrection and the call to Christian Believers and all that stuff.'

Tyra chuckled. 'Vicars can have a nasty habit of mentioning God from time to time,' she murmured. It was meant as gentle teasing, but she felt that she'd lost the knack for that over the years and wondered if it had sounded sarcastic. So she pushed on with, 'Your dad didn't have Max doing it then?'

'No, but I think that probably would have been better.'

'How is he... Your dad, I mean?'

'That's a tough one!' Elin tried to answer honestly. Though she didn't really know how to put her misgivings into words. 'You know he's always been kind of... fragile, right?'

'Yes, I suppose so.'

Elin sighed. 'Well... He's just so... miserable. It knocked him when Mum went, but they've stayed good friends. And he really seemed on a high when the record went into the charts and he started rehearsals with Max and Danny. He was writing new music and everything. And then all this with Grandad has just floored him.... It must have been traumatic, finding him like that. But he doesn't seem to be showing any sign of picking up from it. And he's refusing to talk to anyone professional... You know, like a counsellor or somebody like that. I thought he might be a bit more back to normal after the funeral, but he isn't. I'll be honest, I'm worried about him.'

Out of the corner of her eye, she could see that Tyra was listening. She waited to see if she would say anything, but she didn't.

'You know him better than anyone, other than Mum,' she said and paused again.

Then, deciding that her aunt just wasn't good at responding to oblique references, she tried a direct question. 'What do you think could be going on for him?'

Finally, Tyra looked like she might answer. Though the shrug she prefaced her words with didn't bode well.

'I haven't seen your dad for more than forty years,' she said. 'I only know the person he was up to his mid-twenties. Up till then, he had a terrible relationship with our father. And I can't imagine it will have changed much after I'd gone. All your dad ever wanted was for your grandad to love him. But for our father, your dad was a lost cause. He was everything your grandad hated to see in a man. Your dad was sensitive and gentle and kind. All those things that must have made him a lovely father to you. But he could never win with your grandad, no matter how hard he tried. He was always just a 'sissy' and a 'cry-baby' in the old man's eyes.'

Elin took this in. It made a lot of sense to her. She'd seen it.

'Is that why Mum disliked him so much?' she asked. 'Because of the way he treated Dad?'

'I guess,' said Tyra, busying herself with unwrapping the Danish pastry.

Elin decided to leave it for now. She was starting to know when the elder Alströms were choosing to keep the truth from her. And she knew that she'd get nowhere pushing her aunt about things if she was determined to keep them secret.

Sixteen

The hall of Max's church was typical of its kind. A large, echoey room with a high ceiling and tall windows. There was a wooden floor, pitted with the imprints of 1960's stiletto heels. Stacked plastic chairs and folded trestle tables were pushed against walls that urgently needed a re-paint. The skirting boards and doors were glossed in a dark blue rarely seen outside institutions.

The stage had ancient rose velvet curtains and a piano. It also, on this occasion, held Max's battered drum kit, plus the electronic drum controller that had replaced the various percussive oddities he used to hump around to gigs. Danny had brought his bass guitars and pedals. Amps and entrail-like swirls of cable left little room to walk in safety. Three microphones on stands looked like wallflowers at a youth club dance.

It was Friday, twelve thirty. Max and Danny were sitting on the edge of the stage smoking roll-ups. 'Tiff', a twenty two year old rap artist, sat beside them, but upwind of their smoke. She'd tried tutting and nodding in the direction of the 'No Smoking' signs, but the men were sunk too deep in gloom to care. She was the only female vocalist to respond to the handwritten notice Danny had put up at his recording studio. And now she was multi-tasking, curling her hair around the forefinger of her left hand while texting her boyfriend, Chainy, with the dexterous thumb of the right.

Danny, in his embarrassment, thought she was probably complaining about him. Telling some friend or other how she wished she'd never got involved. And what a pair of old losers he and Max were. In fact, she was reminding Chainy that they needed washing up liquid when he called at the supermarket on his way home. But all the other stuff had gone through her mind too.

'We'll have to hide these pretty smartish if the Church Warden comes sniffing around,' said Max, waving his rollie. 'He's desperate for an excuse to dob me in to the Bishop.'

Danny nodded morosely and flicked ash into the old tobacco tin he always carried for the purpose.

'Looks like we can write Pete off,' he said. 'Are you sure you told Helen the right day and time?'

'Yes!'

'And place...? You told her it was gonna be here... I mean?'

'Yes Dan. All that!'

'Do you think she might have forgotten to tell him.'

Max gave him a withering look.

'Sorry!' he said, blowing a thin stream of smoke up towards the ceiling. 'It's just not... like him... you know? I mean, the man was always so freaking anal about everything.'

Max shook his head. 'He's not been the same since Helen left,' he said sadly. 'She always held him together you know.'

'Mm!' Danny shook his head slowly. 'So... What now?'

Max shuffled a little, like a guilty schoolboy. 'I told her we were thinking of carrying on without him,' he admitted.

Danny looked startled at this. 'What the hell did you do that for man?'

'I don't know. I was trying to motivate him, I guess.'

'Well... that was a great success, wasn't it!' Dan gestured at the empty hall. He shook his head and tutted in disbelief.

'Sorry mate!'

They both sighed and stubbed the ends of their roll-ups into Danny's tin. He clicked the lid on and put it in the inside pocket of his bomber jacket. 'Guess we may as well get this lot back in the van,' he said. 'And get that gig cancelled. I suppose a bereavement's as good an excuse as any.'

He hopped off the stage. Tiff looked up, relieved. She put her phone away in readiness for legging it. But Max stayed put.

'But is it such a bad idea?' he asked. 'You know, getting some more guys together and going ahead.'

Danny looked at him as if he'd taken leave of his senses.

'Nobody's gonna come to see us,' he said. 'We knew already that the Gays wouldn't be bothered without Tyra.... I mean... No offence Tiff...'

She shrugged. Becoming a Gay icon wasn't high on her priority list.

'Well... no, but.... We might get a whole new crowd. What about all those Scandi-noir fans.'

'Sure man... Without the Scandis?!'

Max looked crestfallen at this. 'I suppose you've got a point there,' he said.

It took a lot to get Danny going, but now he'd got started, he was on a roll…

'And what about the name?' he demanded. 'How would that work without the freaking Alströms?'

'Yeah!' Max confessed gloomily. 'Helen *did* point that one out to me.'

'Maybe you were thinking you could persuade her to come and bash a tambourine for us? Though we'd have to disband then if she reverts to her maiden name after the divorce.'

'Well, there's no need to be sarky mate, it was just a thought.'

Danny glared at him. 'You're an imbecile man. Pete's probably on the phone to his lawyers even as we speak.'

Max's face dropped. 'Oh jeez… er… I mean… sorry Lord…' he said, 'I hadn't thought of that. I'll phone now and cancel the gig. And I'll give Helen a bell too… I'd better tell her I was only joking.'

Tiff was beyond bored now. She wasn't that keen on Alstrom's music anyway. And she knew a complete non-starter when she saw one.

'I'm out of here,' she said, hopping off the stage.

'Yeah… Sorry Tiff! It could have been a goer.'

'No probs Dan. But you'll still do the bass tracks for my demo, right?'

'A deal's a deal Tiff.'

'Cool! See you at the studio then, Monday evening.'

'Sure, see you then.'

The two men watched glumly as she slouched out of the hall, all hoodie, and baggy arsed jeans.

'I'm not sure she was right for us anyway,' said Max, with a sigh.

Danny thought of his long-ago girlfriend, Susan, Alstrom's first singer, and weakest link.

'Beggars can't be choosers mate. At least she was in tune. Which is more than could be said for that old bird of mine back in the day. Anyway, we tried. Let's get this stuff in the van and go home.'

'I guess *we* may as well go home too then,' said Elin behind them.

They spun round in unison.

Tyra stepped hesitantly out of the shadowy side entrance to the hall, not sure of the reception she'd get from her two old bandmates.

-0-0-0-

But she needn't have worried.

After several minutes of hugging and squealing from Max, a slow affectionate shoulder punch from Danny, and polite lies about how none of them had changed a bit on all sides, Tyra extricated herself and introduced her niece.

'I think you've all heard lots about each other, but I don't think you've ever actually met Pete's daughter, Elin?'

Max's eyes lit up. 'Ah, I remember seeing this lovely young lady at the funeral. But her father never introduced us!'

Tyra tutted.

'God, are you surprised Max? How on earth have you escaped the wrath of the 'Me Too' movement?'

'I'll tell you exactly how!' he said, pretending to be affronted. 'Those guys are complete and utter misogynistic bastards…. I… on the other hand love women with every fibre of my being. A bit like you… if I remember correctly.'

He winked playfully, as he said this, and Tyra felt herself growing hot with embarrassment. She'd have preferred her ancient misdemeanours not to be discussed in front of her niece. It was all a bit of a blur, anyway, to be honest, though she wondered sometimes if she'd fallen more into the misogynistic bastard camp than any of her male bandmates ever had.

Elin sensed her discomfort. 'No sign of Dad then?' she asked, quickly, changing the subject.

The two men shook their heads.

'Oh well… Maybe next time!' Elin's voice took on the false brightness of someone who's just accidentally mentioned the elephant in the room. 'How about I go get lunch for us while you all have a catch up? I think I saw a Costa down the road.'

Whether her father eventually turned up or not, she was hoping to make herself indispensable. And she'd always believed the old saying that the way to men's hearts is through their stomachs.

The chorus of approval all round suggested that her plan was getting off to a good start.

Seventeen

Helen's mobile was on silent, but when it flashed with Elin's name, she answered immediately.

'Hi sweetheart. Is everything ok?' In the background she could hear the unmistakable sounds of a coffee bar. The hum of voices, the clatter of cups, and what sounded tantalisingly like the hiss of an espresso machine. 'Sounds like you're having a coffee break. Can you get me one?' This was a long standing joke between them, no matter how far away from each other they might be.

Elin laughed. 'Cappuccino on its way. Remember to open the window! I've just dropped Auntie Tyra off at band practice, and now I'm getting us all some lunch at Costa.'

Silence dragged out across the airwaves. She wondered if she'd lost the connection.

'It's great, isn't it? She arrived this morning. From Spain.'

In her ears, Helen heard her own blood pulsing, like surf on a shingle beach.

She found that she had to clear her throat to get the words out.

'That's quite a surprise,' she said croakily, staring at the tree outside her window to ground herself. She thought, inconsequentially, that it was starting to look fuzzy with leaf buds. Behind it, the sky was a brilliant powder blue. 'Is your dad there too?'

'No, sorry! He's in a bad way, isn't he? But I'm hoping, if we can keep the band going, we might be able to tempt him back in a week or two.'

Helen noticed that her hands were shaking. She sat down.

'Well, maybe. Fingers crossed! Where's Tyra staying? Not at the old house, surely?'

'No... I asked her to stay with me and Dave. But she wouldn't. She's booked in at the Value Lodge near us. She says she likes hotel rooms.'

This was true. Though Helen had forgotten until now. She could feel her heart hammering in her chest. She felt herself growing sweaty.

'I can bring her round to see you later if you'd like... I don't suppose the band will be able to do much in the way of practising today. They've got to be out before 3pm.'

Ah yes... The Over Sixties Art Club, thought Helen, remembering her conversation with Max. Then, 'No!' she said, sounding firmer than she'd meant to. 'It's probably not a good idea. I'll phone you tonight though, ok? See how it's all going...'

'Shall I give Auntie Tyra your love?'

Helen heard and pretended she hadn't. She hung up the call, leaving the question unanswered. Then she sat down on the sofa, waiting for her heart to slow to its normal pace.

Tyra had come home....

'Forty years too late,' she said out loud.

She wondered, if she said it often enough, if she might be able to convince herself that she meant it.

Eighteen

They weren't going to be headliners at the gig. Just support for local heavy metal band 'Rats in the Stairwell'.

They'd be expected to perform what had now become known as 'The Fördömelse Theme', of course. It had, after all, just officially made them One Hit Wonders. Other than that, no-one cared. As a band of seventies has-beens, they were hardly likely to upstage the bare chested, mane-shaking, vocal-belting lads of the main act. And that was all that really mattered.

They'd done it all so many times before. Night after night, for years. There had been the miserable times when the audiences were mean and impatient, when the equipment blew up, or the van broke down. And nights when there were rumours of A&R guys scouting, or when the music papers were reviewing the main band and might just give them a mention too. But it was always the same. Get out there. Get the audience nodding their heads a little if they could be bothered shutting up long enough to listen. Sell a few autographed home produced cassettes of their songs if they were lucky. Then make way for the true stars of the show.

They'd suffered the penalties of getting carried away and forgetting their place in that hierarchy. They'd had their tyres slashed, money withheld, and a head butt for Danny in one particularly nasty fight with disgruntled headliners. They'd learned the hard way how to get the balance right.

But with just four weeks now to perfect songs they hadn't sung for forty years, and one of the busiest weeks of the year in Max's day job in the middle of that time, just not making total muppets of themselves would be nice.

'So,' said Max, hopefully. 'You'll do the gig with us?'

'Yeah, I'll play keyboards if Pete doesn't reappear. I've done a bit of playing and mixing in clubs over the years, but not for a while, so I need to warn you, I'm seriously rusty.'

'Oh man…. That's great! And you'll do the vocals too, right?'

In the old Alstrom, Tyra had reluctantly done both, after the tuneless Susan walked out. As far as she was concerned, it had been the beginning of the slippery slope that ended with Peter persuading them all that they'd be better with Tyra up-front and in the spotlight, like Susan had always been.

'God, no! I thought Danny had found a singer?'

Tyra remembered all too well how she'd been gradually sucked into being the lead vocalist for the band. She was living in London and Studying Literature at UCL. She had the smallest bedroom in the large Victorian terrace house her parents had bought as an investment, and where she lived rent-free, with Peter, his bandmates, and an endless succession of Max's 'lady friends'.

Playing in Alstrom wasn't part of the original deal. She

was supposed to be focusing on her studies. But their first keyboard player had left, citing 'artistic differences'. And she enjoyed standing in for him. It gave her a bit of 'Street Cred' at university. And she was in her comfort zone in the shadows at the side of the stage with her beloved red Farfisa and Minimoog. It was supposed to be temporary. And nobody had ever mentioned anything about singing. There'd never even been a microphone anywhere near her.

But then Susan had decided to ditch her hapless boyfriend less than an hour before a gig. 'Apparently I'm a loser and a pot head,' he'd said glumly, through a fog of suspiciously sweet smelling smoke. This was a huge blow to the band. Given the quality of Susan's vocals, it was a blessing that most of the time she was just fluttering around the stage in cheesecloth and patent leather boots looking decorative. Most of Alstrom's work was instrumental, in the same vein as Peter's musical idols, The Nice, ELP and Ekseption. But some of his epic compositions did have words. Particularly, his interpretation of the old Nordic saga Beowulf.

Tyra remembered how they'd all turned and looked at her then, in exactly the way Danny and Max were looking at her now. Alstrom had always had a female vocalist. It wasn't something you saw very often back in those days. And Susan's departure, no matter how off-key she might have been, had left them without one of their most important assets.

It was Peter who'd voiced what all three were thinking. 'You could do it Ty,' he'd said. 'Easy as falling off a log. You've got a great voice. And you know the songs.'

She could still remember the terror his words had ignited in her.

'I can't sing in front of an audience!' she'd protested, looking to the other two to back her up.

But she could see, through the haze of Danny's smoke and her fear, that they were both nodding encouragingly at her.

'Well, it's time you got over this silly stage fright thing of yours,' said Peter, forgetting for a moment how hard he'd always found it to conquer any of his own demons. 'You do it already. I've seen you, singing away there to yourself… The only difference would be having a mic in front of you. Please Tyra… Please… For the sake of the band! Just for tonight, till we get a replacement for Susan. You'll be fine. Look, I can get you something for your nerves. You'll be great. I promise.'

They never did get a replacement for Susan. Though eventually, they found Brian, and Tyra was stuck centre stage where she had never wanted to be. She hated people watching her. It consumed her with an all pervasive terror that she had never managed to conquer. But she was too talented for Peter to resist. And with a good vocalist at last, the band had strayed, not always gently, from their instrumental roots to a more vocal-heavy sound.

Peter got her something for her nerves.

She thought it helped at the time.

But she was older now. And wiser….

And Max still had a pleading look about him. Like he believed he'd grind her down eventually if he stayed looking like a sweet little lost puppy for long enough.

'Seriously Max, I can't!' she said, firmly. 'I'll do some backing vocals if I have to. But I can't and I won't sing lead. I had to get off my face to do it. It took me years to get straight. And I'm not prepared to do that anymore.'

Danny sighed. 'I suppose we'll have to get Tiff back then.'

Max shook his head. 'I don't know man. There wasn't a lot of chemistry there.'

'Well, what option do we have?'

Elin was back from Costa. She'd heard most of the exchange, though the trio had been too absorbed in their discussion to notice her return. She wondered how Tyra's drinking didn't class as 'getting off her face'. But she'd long since given up trying to understand her parents' generation. And more urgently, she sensed that her plans for literary fame were about to go up in smoke.

'I'll do it!' she said, in a fit of panic.

Max's eyes lit up.

'But can you sing?' asked Danny, doubtfully. His experience of his long-ago girlfriend had taught him that people weren't always their own best judges in that regard.

Elin put the take-out coffees and panini bags on the edge of the stage.

'Of course I can sing!' she said. 'I'm an Alström.'

'Hallelujah!' Max forgot for a moment that he was Anglican and punched the air like a fully-fledged Gospel Revivalist. 'Looks like we've got ourselves a band!'

-0-0-0-

'I need to get myself kitted out,' said Tyra, when Max had finished doing his happy dance. 'I don't even own a keyboard anymore. Unless you count the one on the 'Music Studio' App on my mobile phone.'

She had no illusions about the enormity of the task ahead

of her. She was rusty as hell. And she could barely remember the songs.

Danny's good natured face lit up at the opportunity to fix the problem. 'No worries!' he said. 'Come back to the studio with me after we've packed up here, and I'll get you sorted. How about we agree the Set List now, so you know what to be practising, Then, maybe we can reconvene tomorrow? How does that sound to everyone?'

-0-0-0-

They regrouped at the hall, the next night, setting up their equipment while a frisky looking Salsa class outstayed their welcome, chattering and flirting around the edges of the room.

A burst of heavy metal drumming from Max sent them scurrying for the exit.

'Hah! Learnt that one from Keith Moon,' he chuckled, when the last of the dancers had disappeared.

Elin had left Dave having a peaceful night in with Dido on his lap. He was supposed to be marking homework. But she knew that as soon as she was out of earshot, he'd be watching an early Jean-Claude Van Damme film, or something of the same ilk, on the Movies for Men channel.

Tyra had been quiet in the car. She'd spent the day in her hotel room finding her way around the keyboard, controller, and laptop that Danny had lent her from his studio. She'd seemed uncharacteristically excited when he piled the kit into carry bags for her at first. But she was subdued again now.

And Elin was raring to go. She'd always loved the

limelight, even as a little girl in her best frock at her primary school Christmas concert. She'd sung 'I saw Mummy kissing Santa Claus' (an ironic song, she realised now, judging from the state of her parents' marriage). She'd forgotten some of her lines. But the 'aww's of the audience had taught her that forgetting lines could be just as good as remembering them. And the sight of her mum and dad standing up to applaud at the end had been better than all the birthdays in the world.

She thought how strange it was that people could interpret the excitement of being on stage so differently. For Tyra, it seemed to be a source of crippling self-consciousness and dread. Yet, for her father, it had been the only thing that ever fully pulled him from his baseline state of depression. This made it all the more unfathomable to her that he had dropped out of the band now. He'd been elated when he'd first thought of the reunion. But grief was an unpredictable emotion. And the relationship between her father and grandfather had never been an easy one.

They'd agreed a Set List, as Danny had suggested. Kicking off with Tyra's edgy LGBT anthem 'Stonewall is Coming', and ending with 'You Watching Me,' the Fördömelse theme that most of their audience would be waiting for.

Tyra had had a little fun with Max, teasing him about 'Stonewall'. Are you sure you're not worried about people thinking you're a 'poof?' she asked, reminding him of some long ago homophobia.

'I was a Neanderthal then,' said Max.

'We were all ruddy Neanderthal's,' said Danny, with feeling.

This appeared to be their final word on the subject.

'One, two, three, four,' Max counted them in with his drumsticks, Danny nodded in his own world somewhere in the depths, and Tyra's old Farfisa lines, re-imagined through the alchemy of the magical software on the laptop, rumbled ominously, like a thunderstorm gathering in the distance. Elin moved closer to the microphone, cupped it with her hands and sang.

Nineteen

Hidden in the shadow of the side door, Helen listened to the staggering stops and starts of their playing. She had always loved the songs of Alstrom. And it felt unexpectedly poignant to hear them in her daughter's voice. She could hear Tyra too, in the harmonies, weaving around the lead. Her heart flipped at the familiar sound, though she chided herself for being so stupid. Tyra had walked out on her years ago. And she'd come back purely for the band. It was madness to imagine this was any more than that.

And yet, tonight, here she was. Listening in the shadows. Ready to disappear, unseen, at any moment.

She'd tried to stay away. She'd planned a night in her own flat, eating pasta, maybe with a glass of red wine, and an old black and white movie on Freeview. But then Elin had phoned, excited to tell her that she'd taken on the vocals and they'd be rehearsing that night. And she'd known that she longed with all her heart, to see Tyra.

Now, keeping half an ear towards the stage, ready to slip into the room behind her if anyone decided to go to the kitchen, or toilet, she remembered the first time she'd heard Tyra sing.

-0-0-0-

It was October 1974. A Friday night. She was tired at the end of a long week, and desperate for the half term holiday. And though she hadn't really admitted it to herself yet, she was starting to wonder if she was growing up and leaving Peter behind. It wasn't a constant feeling. She still had times when she felt that she loved him. And she knew it wasn't possible to keep the initial passion of any relationship going forever. But her wealthy 'boyfriend' (and even the term was starting to feel like something she'd outgrown) was living off a sizeable Trust Fund, and dreaming rock star dreams, while she was grappling with the brutal reality of Inner City teaching. And the distance between those two existences was starting to take its toll.

She'd confided her ambivalence (about the gig, and, indirectly, the relationship) that night to her flatmate, Bridget, who had been quick to suggest staying in with a bottle of Blue Nun and a 'Chinese'. And she'd been sorely tempted to phone Peter and excuse herself with a headache that wasn't entirely fictional.

But in the end, she'd left Bridget in front of the TV, and talked herself into going. She could sleep in the next day after all. She had all weekend for marking and lesson prep. And she knew that Peter would be hurt if she didn't turn up.

The gig was in the Union Bar of one of the London Polytechnics. She couldn't remember which one. There had been so many colleges, universities, clubs, and pubs. So many small stages and audiences more interested in talking than listening. The bar area was crowded with wall to wall denim and long hair. And it smelt of smoke and beer, like they all did. The industrial strength, tight weave carpet was tacky, with years of spillages and a scattering of crisps and Pork Scratchings.

The stage was over to the right with a dancefloor in front.

A disco ball swept thin speckles of light over everything, and flashing lamps at the front of the stage threatened to turn her hovering headache into a migraine.

She thought again that she could just turn round and go home. But she knew that Peter would need reassurance when the gig was over. So, she struggled to the bar and bought a half pint of lager and lime and trailed across the dancefloor to one of the chairs at its edge, close to the stage.

Unusually, and probably because of budgetary constraints at the Student Union, Alstrom were the headline act that night. But no-one seemed very excited about seeing them. And there wasn't exactly a stampede when a greasy haired young man from 'Ents' introduced them.

'Laydees and Gentle-men... Please give a big hand for our band tonight...' He blinked in the spotlight and misread the name from a crumpled scrap of paper in his hand. 'Al's Room.'

Helen applauded enthusiastically, but she was the only one. People continued shouting orders and laughing loudly at the bar. One or two of the students began straggling down to the dancefloor as the band filed on stage. She picked out Peter's rippling shoulder length blond hair first. Then Max settling himself behind his drum kit. Danny shrugging into the shoulder strap of his bass. Then playing a few notes. Adjusting the sound a little on his monitor. And Tyra slipping in quietly in the shadows, hiding herself away, as always, behind the keyboards.

Their opening tracks were instrumental. Peter liked to give them quirky titles like 'Hayden Seek', 'The Bachinside Toccata', and 'Rondo Alla Turkish Baths'. As always, his puns fell flat with the audience.

But a few of the people at the bar pricked up their ears at the familiarity of it all, and shuffled down to the dancefloor, still clutching their pint glasses, drawn to a sound that reminded them of the bigger bands they played at home. They stood, by themselves, or in pairs, or small clumps, quiet now, getting in the zone, doing the strange zombie head-nod that characterised the audiences of the genre. If they were really 'blown-away' by the music as it reached its climax, they might rock the whole of their upper bodies and punch the air. Though there were never many places for them to do that in an Alstrom set.

Helen sipped her lager and lime and drifted as the music washed over her. She'd heard it all so many times before, and she could hardly keep her eyes open. The headache was intensifying, aggravated, no doubt, by the alcohol, throbbing miserably, along with Danny's bass. But she was puzzled by the absence of Susan. Tyra on keyboards, was teasing out the opening riff to Peter's beloved 'Beowulf', a faint murmur of the Gregorian chant 'Dies Irae', played slow and low, introducing the first movement. In movements two and three there would be opportunities for all three 'boys' in the band to indulge in a lengthy solo. But this first part was tighter, and the few lyrics there were had an unusual empathy for the monster.

And still, there had been no grand entrance from the vocalist.

Helen had always seen Susan as the weakest link of the band. And Susan, who had a futile crush on Peter, wasn't too keen on Helen either.

But none of that was relevant to tonight's performance. Susan should have been on stage by now, dancing and looking good in some floaty outfit that showed her figure to best advantage. Sometimes Helen, who, encouraged by Bridget, had started to read 'Spare Rib', thought that the Alstrom vocalist's true purpose was to give the audience something to fantasise about when they got home that night to their lonely student digs.

Still, no-one on stage seemed worried by her absence.

Helen wondered if she was ill, and Peter was going to sing the vocals. He could do a passable countertenor when he set his mind to it.

She expected him to step up to the mic as the music built to the first sung words, a description of the abode of the monster Grendel...

Outcast to joy and stranger to pleasure... Banished forever from warm hearth and from home...

It was the first time she'd heard it sung in tune. Surprised, she scanned the stage. She saw the microphone by Tyra's keys as Peter nodded smugly over his guitar.

Tyra continued, her clear, pure notes transforming the music.

On wind harrowed headlands and loneliest fen deeps...
Feared by the fearless ones, there Grendel roams...

Helen caught movement out of the corner of her eye, and turning, saw a small, but steady trickle of drinkers drawn towards the stage by her voice.

-0-0-0-

When the concert was over, Helen made her way backstage. The lads were buzzing and swigging Jack Daniels from the bottle. Even Danny was wide-awake with excitement.

Peter flung his arm round Helen's shoulders. 'How's about that then?' he slurred. 'Two encores! We're gonna have to write more freaking songs! Didn't I say Ty'd be brilliant? Didn't I...'

'You did mate,' said Max, obligingly, 'You did! Where is she by the way?'

They all looked around the grubby dressing room with the exaggerated studiousness of people who are half-cut, or stoned, or both.

But Tyra was nowhere to be seen.

'She's prob'ly gone out for a breath o' fresh air,' said Peter. 'Or to the loo... or something. Le's go get the gear off stage. And you too losers can see if you can rustle up a couple of birds. I've got another bottle of this back home.' He kissed the Jack Daniels bottle.

It occurred to Helen that there was rather more passion

in that kiss than anything he'd shown her lately. And she thought it was telling that she wasn't bothered. Just slightly miffed that she was going to be the one driving them all home.... Again.

'I'll go see if I can find Tyra,' she said.

She felt a faint draught coming from the Stage Door before she even noticed that it was ajar. She opened it quietly and peered out into the night.

The band's van was parked a couple of car lengths down the cobbled side street.

By the light of a solitary streetlamp, she could see Tyra leaning against it.

She was throwing up.

Hearing Helen's footsteps behind her, she turned with tear-filled eyes. She blew her nose wretchedly. 'God, I'm sorry! she said. 'Nobody was meant to see that. Whiskey doesn't normally have that effect on me.'

Helen's heart went out to her. 'I guess you don't normally drink it on top of stage fright,' she said gently. Then, when she felt confident that Tyra wasn't about to be sick again, she opened her arms. 'Come here love!'

Tyra moved hesitantly towards her. And when Helen stepped forward, she buried her face in her jacket and clung to her, shivering and ashamed.

'Just for the record,' murmured Helen. 'You were bloody good up there.'

She stroked Tyra's hair, finding herself, unexpectedly wanting to kiss it. The impulse shocked her. It was like the feeling she'd had with Peter, that first night. And with the boy at school who had broken her heart. She told herself she was being stupid. She loved Tyra. But not like that. They were practically sisters by now, after all.

She patted the girl's shoulder gently to hint that the hug was over.

And told herself she didn't feel bereft as Tyra recoiled from her arms.

'Sorry,' said the kid. 'I must smell pretty gross. I'd better go clean myself up.'

Helen felt panicky then. She wanted to say, 'Don't leave me,' but it would have sounded weird. She reached out instead and grasped Tyra's arm so she couldn't go.

She stared at her in the yellow light of the streetlamp.

'Also, just for the record,' she said. 'Did Peter give you any of his pills tonight?'

Tyra's edginess at the question told her all she needed to know before she answered. 'Just some diazepam,' she said. Then, defending Peter, as always, 'Nothing serious.'

Helen made a mental note to 'have a word' with Peter when he was sober enough to listen to her.

And then the door was flung open, and Max and Danny appeared with the band's cart piled high with equipment. They looked even drunker than before.

'So, there you are Ty!' slurred Max. 'Jeez, some mucky bastard's thrown up all over the back tyre! The gig wasn't that bad, for goodness sake!'

They all laughed at that. Because they knew the gig had really been very good.

-0-0-0-

Now, in 2019, listening to the banter on stage felt like being transported back to those days...

Without Peter, Max seemed to have taken on the boss role.

'Very nice!' he said, when they'd got all the way through without any of them losing the plot. 'That should get us off to a good start. There are bound to be one or two crazy old lezzies turning up to letch at Ty...'

He paused for Tyra's protest at his deliberate political incorrectness. But she decided not to dignify it with a response.

'Ok then... What did we decide on next Dan?'

Tyra's voice broke in, sending shivers down Helen's spine.

'How about we have a quick break?' she asked. 'You guys could have a fag. And I could make us all a cup of tea in the kitchen.'

There was a general murmur of assent and drink orders. And panicked by the thought of Tyra heading for the steps at the side of the stage, Helen dove into the room she'd earmarked as a bolthole and pulled the door behind her. It was dark in there and she was afraid to draw attention to herself by turning on the light. But as her eyes grew accustomed to the gloom, she started to make out a piano stacked with music, and a circle of plastic chairs. In the kitchen, next door, she could hear Tyra clattering around, filling a kettle with water, hunting in cupboards for mugs.

She had just pressed her ear against the wall, drinking in those faint, domestic sounds, when suddenly, the door was flung open, nearly scaring the life out of her. A short, crow-like, and clearly irate figure stood in the doorway, silhouetted against the light of the corridor outside.

'Hah!' hissed the Church Warden, with prurient outrage.

'I saw you come skulking in here young lady. I warned the Bishop that this would happen. 'Groupies', I said. 'The place will be crawling with them. You mark my words!' And here you are. Merely the advance guard, I'm sure. Come on now. We'll not have any of those disreputable shenanigans in here.'

He gestured dramatically with his head in the direction of the front door, and Helen followed him meekly. She couldn't decide whether to be mortified or amused. Certainly, she couldn't remember the last time she'd been referred to as 'young'. Or a 'groupie' either. Though occasionally people had taken her for the latter, in the old days, when she'd been 'with the band'.

She kept her head down as she passed the serving hatch to the kitchen.

Tyra, watching the officious little warden bustling by, thought that the woman with him looked a lot like Helen. But she was so used to seeing her in strangers all the time, she barely gave it a second thought.

Twenty

It was 2am by the time Elin got home. She was still buzzing with the excitement of the rehearsal and longing to tell Dave all about it. But he was spark out on the sofa with his arm round Dido and both were snoring fit to wake the dead.

'Good job I'm not a burglar!' she muttered as she went into the kitchen to appease her sudden craving for toast and tea.

She perched at the breakfast bar in the kitchen, munching through hot buttery toast with just a smidgeon of Marmite, and wondered how she was ever going to sleep.

She could see how Tyra, coping with her agonising performance anxiety on top of late nights and surging adrenalin could so easily have succumbed to drugs to manage it all.

It was easy enough to see Tyra as an addict. She'd seen her drinking, after all. And she'd seen and heard the evidence in those old recordings. But Elin liked her aunt. She was quiet and introspective and maybe even, though it seemed an odd thing to think of the older generation, a little shy. Behind the keyboards, she was focused, and self-critical when she got it wrong. She was also, Elin thought, surprisingly lacking in ego.

In the car, on the way back to the Value Lodge, she'd seemed pleased and a little sleepy.

'I think it's going to be ok,' she'd said.

Elin wasn't sure whether she was talking about the concert, or life in general.

'Of course it is!' she'd replied. 'It's going to be brilliant.'

'I wish your father would join us.'

So, she was talking about the concert…

'I'll try asking him again, now you're back. Or maybe you could call round and see him. I think he was disappointed that you weren't at the funeral.'

'Yes,' said Tyra. 'I imagine he was.'

Elin heard the full-stop in Tyra's tone.

Outside, the tree-lined streets were quiet and dark. Minutes ticked by as Elin tried to think of something else to say. She'd always felt uncomfortable with silence.

'Have you written any new music while you've been abroad?'

'Yes, some. In my head mainly. I'll see what you all think if we can get the old stuff sounding ok. I guess Max and Danny might have some new stuff too. And your Dad.'

Elin shook her head. 'I doubt that.'

'Well… he may surprise you.'

Tyra stared out of the window as they passed a row of shops, a Post Office and local Co-op, all closed. Elin wondered if she might be looking for somewhere to buy booze, though she didn't say so, and it was too late anyway.

'What's the story with you and Mum?' she asked suddenly, unable to stifle her curiosity any longer.

Tyra paused just long enough for her to know she was about to be fed a line.

'There is no story. We always got on ok.'

'So, why doesn't she ever talk about you?'

'I've no idea. Maybe she's angry with me for messing up the band... She probably thinks I let your dad down.... And she'd be right... Oh look, here's the hotel now.'

Elin pulled into the car park and stopped by the front door.

'I'll help you in with your stuff.'

'No, it's ok, I can manage.'

'Why don't you come for Sunday lunch with me and Dave tomorrow? Or should I say, later. I guess it's Sunday already.'

'Thanks... That's very kind. But I'm quite tired. I think I'll just get something at the pub next door.'

'You could meet our dog, Dido.'

'That would be great... Another time.'

Tyra got out and gathered the bags with the keyboard and laptop from the back seat where she'd secured them with the rear seat belts.

Elin felt wretched for mentioning her mother. It seemed to have shoved Tyra back into her shell.

'I'll collect you for rehearsal on Monday then... 10am?'

'Sure, I'll be waiting here.'

'You won't do another runner, will you?' God, why on earth had she just asked that?

'No, I promise.'

Elin watched Tyra out of her rear view mirror, illuminated by the lights of the hotel. She waved, then turned wearily towards reception with the keyboard under one arm and the laptop case slung over her shoulder.

She looked lost. And terribly alone.

Twenty-One

SUNDAY 7TH APRIL 2019

Helen and Bridget always had Sunday lunch at the Five Acres Pub. The Yorkshire Puddings from the Serve Yourself Buffet were invariably rubbery and the 'roasties' were cold. But it was cheap and cheerful and within easy walking distance of home for both of them. So, they could share a bottle of wine, take as long as they wanted, and egg each other on to indulge in gloriously unhealthy desserts like Triple Toffee Sundae, or Gin and Tonic Pannacotta, to their heart's content.

When Helen still lived with Peter, he'd deeply resented his wife's desertion at what he saw as prime 'family time'. But when Bridget lost her partner Deidre, Sundays had been the best day for them to meet. They'd still been working during the week. Elin had, long since, left home. And Sundays, alone, were miserable for Bridget. Now they could have switched to a weekday and enjoyed pensioners rates with the other Golden Oldies. But they'd agreed that the money saved wouldn't compensate for declaring themselves that ancient.

So, they'd decided to stick with Sundays. Until they were 80… at least.

When Helen was still with Peter, she'd tried to make it up to him when she got home. She'd tried telling him anecdotes about the people in the pub, until she realised he had no interest in hearing them. And she'd make nice things for him for his tea to keep him happy. But he never was.

And now Helen could meet anyone she liked, anytime she liked. She still hadn't quite got used to that heady sense of freedom. But she loved it.

As usual, the pub was packed with families who liked a bargain and didn't want to cook. The air hummed with loud chatter interspersed with sudden sharp gusts of laughter and an occasional wail from a baby who would have preferred the peace and quiet of home.

The 'Dessert of the Day' was Sherry Trifle. It was rich and creamy and probably full of air and E numbers. The two old friends didn't care though. They were giggling at Helen's account of her misunderstanding with the Church Warden.

'Well, you floozy!' spluttered Bridget, wiping tears of laughter from her eyes. 'I bet he thought you were after Max.'

Helen cracked up again at this. 'God, don't! He's already offered me his services if I get lonely. He's a menace!'

'Oh please let me un-hear that!!!!'

Helen rolled her eyes. 'I know! My thoughts precisely!'

'So?' Bridget asked, when she'd finally stopped chuckling. 'I may have missed a vital part of the story here! But why didn't you just go in the front door like any normal person? And say, 'Hi Tyra, it's good to see you!'

'God love… You know why.'

It was as if a blanket had fallen on their mirth. Bridget looked across the table, and Helen could see the concern in her friend's soft grey eyes. She'd followed Helen's entanglement with the Alströms for many years. Indeed, very briefly, she'd been entangled with them herself. She'd rarely seen it bring much in the way of happiness for any of them.

'Maybe *you* should look her up while she's here,' said Helen, seriously.

'Oh-no!' Bridget shook her head as she drained her glass and refilled it. 'That ship has well and truly sailed.'

'You were quite into her at one time.... if I remember correctly.'

'No sweetheart. We were both into *you*. Though I can't deny, she was very sexy when she was younger.'

Helen laughed. 'She was, wasn't she?'

'I don't suppose you've dared ask Elin what she looks like now?'

'I dread to think... And that's right.... But you may have given me a conversational opening there... 'Your Auntie Bridget wants to know if Tyra's still got it'.... I'm sure she'd be thrilled if I asked. She's been trying to get you fixed up for the past three years. Do you remember when she invited Dave's mum's gay stepsister for Christmas dinner?'

'Oh my God! Hairy toes and hiking sandals, plus postman's shorts and a Christmas jumper!'

'And don't forget the stalker-like obsession with Julia Roberts.'

They both shook their heads at the memory of Elin's clumsy attempts at matchmaking.

'Seriously though. I think you could have been in there if you'd played your cards right.'

'Nope.... If Julia Roberts is her thing then I'm way too butch for her. And anyway, stop trying to change the subject.... I think you need to speak to Tyra. If only to get closure. Seriously.'

'I don't think she'll want to speak to me.'

'Don't be daft. She's always been crazy about you.'

'She had a funny way of showing it.'

'Well, yes. Sometimes people do show things in funny ways. Look... If losing Deidre has taught me one thing, it's that time runs out. Sometimes much sooner than we think. And sometimes we regret the risks we didn't take. What's the worst thing that can happen? She breaks your heart again? So what! You know you can survive that. Give yourself the chance to make things right. She's come back, hasn't she? And knowing Tyra, I can't imagine that's only for the band.'

This was a long speech for Bridget. And Helen knew it was heartfelt.

She leaned forward and squeezed her friend's hand affectionately.

'I'll think about it,' she said.

Bridget grinned, knowing when she was being fobbed off. 'And if you decide against it, well... hell... you could always give Max a ring!'

They both spluttered with laughter again at the idea of that. And with the serious business out of the way, they turned their attention properly to the trifle.

-0-0-0-

Sometimes Tyra thought she was too much like her mother for her own good.

She'd never looked even remotely like Kristina, so everyone had always compared her to her dad. 'A chip off the old block,' they'd say, without really bothering to get to know her.

But Tyra was nothing like Isak. He was a liar and a bully. He took what he could, whenever he could. He was a vengeful man. He would do anything to survive.

And then, of course, there were his perversions....

Isak was a voyeur. The awful creeping suspicion had been growing even before she found him in Helen's bedroom that night. And after that, alerted to how he was, she'd noticed him heading for the library, next to the bathroom, when female guests were in there. She'd found his peephole at the back of one of the bookshelves, behind his copy of 'The Canterbury Tales'. And she remembered the glint of what she now knew must have been binoculars in the window of her father's study too, in the summer holidays when she had schoolfriends staying, playing badminton, or sunbathing in the garden.

She'd never known how much her mother really knew about any of that.

But the public face of her parents' marriage was the image that Isak wanted to portray.

The supremely talented golden couple with their beautiful home and sweet kids.

If they'd inhabited the era of Hello magazine, they'd have been regulars within its pages.

Only the inhabitants of Renton Hall knew the truth about the Alström marriage. Isak's insatiable need to be admired and attended to. And the darkness that lurked beneath the surface.

And yet, Kristina had loved him to the end.

Tyra knew that no matter how flawed he was, her mother never would have been happy without him.

Over the years, she'd tried to understand what would bond someone so irrevocably to a monster. She'd read once that people who stay in such marriages believe that the good part of their partner is the truth. That the rest is just a defence. Tyra had studied enough, meditated enough, read enough, to believe that, at the most fundamental level, this could be true. But at the level of relationship, of safety, and of love, she knew how dangerous such a belief could be.

When she was young, she'd accepted her mother's view of Isak. But as she grew, she could see only too plainly what he was like underneath. His moods came in waves. When he was happy, he was the life and soul of the party. And he could be generous. But when he imagined that things were going badly for him, that's when he would take it out on the people who wouldn't tell anyone. His wife. His son. His agent. All in different ways victims to his endless need to be the centre of everyone's universe.

Tyra couldn't imagine enduring a marriage like that. She couldn't understand a mother ignoring flaws that harmed her children. But, like her mother, she knew that once she'd given her heart, she'd given it for life.

She sighed and popped a couple of Ibuprofen capsules out of their packaging and into her hand.

She was in the pub next door to her hotel. It was much like the one where Helen and Bridget were debating whether to have coffee after their Sherry Trifle. Though she'd balked at the thought of a dried up Sunday Roast and settled instead for Lasagne.

Kids from a party were running around, playing tag amongst the tables, and annoying the older folk who thought that they should be made to sit down and 'behave'. The sound system was playing Frank Sinatra. 'New York. New York.'

She was in pain. Arthritis had crept into her fingers over the years, though she'd only noticed the aching occasionally in Spain. Now, aggravated by a damp English springtime and hours of practice at the keyboard, the joints of her fingers were growling in protest, and she thought wistfully of the days when there was a pill for almost everything. Even ones that temporarily helped her forget her love for Helen.

Frank Sinatra had moved on to singing about how he'd done things his way.

'Bully for you Frank!' she muttered bitterly as she knocked the capsules back with a slug of whiskey.

She stood up wearily. 'No pain, no gain,' she said to herself. It was time for more practice.

-0-0-0-

Finally, realising that she wasn't going to wake up under her own steam, Dave took a mug of tea to Elin.

'Hey sleepy-drawers,' he said, putting the mug on the bedside table and leaning over to kiss the top of her rumpled head. It was the only part he could reach. The rest of her, as always, was completely tucked away under the quilt.

She groaned, like someone with a hangover. Then she lowered the quilt and peeped out at him with one puffy eye.

'What time is it?' she asked, groggily.

He laughed. 'Half past one. Congratulations. You're now officially a Rock Star.'

'Oh, hah hah! God, I feel rough!' Slowly, she eased herself up the bed and pulled the pillow from Dave's side to prop herself up. 'Where's Dido? Has she been out?'

'Of course! We've both been up since 7am. We've been for a walk in the woods. And now she's having her afternoon nap. What the hell happened last night? I hope your Auntie Tyra hasn't been plying you with illegal substances.'

'Nope. Unless you count sleep deprivation. I came home buzzing and didn't manage to drop off till 5am.' She reached for the mug and took a long, grateful slurp.

Dave made himself comfortable on the side of the bed.

'How did it go?'

'Good, I think. Tyra's a bit rusty. But she hasn't played for years.'

'D'you still like her?'

'Yes, very much. She's not a bit like Dad. But I think she's kind of sweet.'

'D'you think you'll be ready in time for the gig.'

'Hopefully. We'll be able to get a few more sessions in this week. Then Max will be full-on vicaring over Easter. So, you and me and Dido will be able to have a bit of 'us' time during the school holidays. And then it's just a few days till the actual concert.'

'Are you enjoying it?'

'Yes, I really am. It's just the biggest buzz!'

'Any goss for your book?' He grinned cheekily and wiggled his eyebrows.

Elin was surprised to find herself shutting down. 'I'm not so sure about that anymore,' she said.

'How come?' Dave looked disappointed.

'I don't think there's very much to tell.'

'Really?'

'Yeah!'

'Are you sure you're not coming over all tribal-loyalty?'

'Maybe… A little. Did you get your marking done?'

'Yes, this morning. Oh, and while I was out with Dido, I called in the Co-op and did a bit of shopping. Spotted that your Grandad's funeral was on the front page of the local rag, so I got you a copy. I'll fetch it for you. Do you fancy a bacon and egg buttie?'

Elin's mouth watered at the thought. It had been a long time since her toast the night before.

'You sure know how to tempt a girl! And then I'm going to have to do some work. I'm sharp up against the deadline for that double glazing company.'

-0-0-0-

The newspaper article was the print copy of the one Peter and Helen had read online.

Elin felt sad as she read the love story of her grandfather and the grandmother she had never met. She remembered the professional photographs of Kristina Alström all over Isak's house. And the snaps Peter treasured, of his mother holding him in his christening robe, building sandcastles with him, helping him blow out the candles on his birthday cake, with a tiny and impossibly cute Tyra by his side.

She had an image of a woman forever young, frozen in time and tragedy.

She'd always been frightened of her grandfather. But she'd never been in any doubt that he had suffered through the loss of Kristina.

She thought that at least now, if there was a heaven, the two were reunited at last. She felt quite emotional as she imagined that. Not knowing that her parents would have been horrified at the thought of it.

But something nagged at her about the end of the piece…

Possibly Peter was going to ask his dad just that when he called round to see him at 7.30pm on the 20th of February. But sadly, he found that his much loved father had died of a stroke, earlier that evening.

At first, she thought they must have got that wrong. But then, she started to wonder.

She checked back through the texts between her father and herself, on the day of Isak's death.

They were time stamped…

4.30pm 'Hi Dad, how're you doing? Do you fancy to come round for tea one night this week?'

4.42pm 'Thank you sweetheart. That would be lovely. I'll look at my diary when I get home. I can't remember which days we've got rehearsals. I'm just parking up at Renton now. Popping in to see your grandad. Should be back home about seven. I'll give you a ring then.'

At 9pm she'd had a call from her father to tell her that Isak was dead. She remembered the time, because she and Dave were washing up after Spaghetti Bolognese and a couple of Now TV episodes of Madam Secretary. And she'd started to feel worried about him.

She looked between the paper and her phone. She thought of her father's mood since the death of Isak. She wondered what her father had done between 4.42 and 7.30 that night. And then she wondered what the hell she was going to do with the questions jangling in her head.

Twenty-Two

Think I'm going crazy, in your madhouse. Am I coming, am I going? Am I going out of my mind?....

Tyra had been practising 'Madhouse Reggae' for over an hour. She was trying to re-fix the music in her head, so that her fingers would trip effortlessly over the keys on the night.

That afternoon, the tripping felt more like the falling flat on your face variety. And her knuckles were howling in pain like a wolf pack at full moon. She'd called at the local mini-market on her way back to her room. She'd bought a bottle of Jack Daniels and a party bag of ice. The level of whiskey was creeping slowly down the bottle. And the ice was melting. And neither of them had given her much relief.

Wearily, she switched the laptop to sleep mode, and threw herself on the bed with its ultra-white, starched quilt cover.

'Madhouse' was the first song of her own that she'd ever felt confident enough to play to the band. The tune came as she tried to reproduce the reggae beats she heard day in day out from Danny's room next door to hers. The lyrics emerged from a dream after watching the old black and white movie 'Gaslight' on TV. Something about the atmosphere of the film had triggered her misgivings about her father. The creepiness of his nocturnal wanderings. And his treatment of her mother and Peter. By the time she was living in the London house she'd fallen into avoiding staying overnight at Renton Hall when her father was there. She knew that hurt her mum. But still, she'd never felt that she could confide in her.

Peter hated the song. He didn't think it fitted the band's 'oeuvre'.

But he was out-voted.

'People are getting bored with all that tinkly twinkly stuff we do,' said Danny. 'I think we should shake it up a bit.'

Peter was distressed at the thought. He had a vision for the band. He'd always been the songwriter and he'd always called the shots. This kind of mutiny was unprecedented. And it felt especially treacherous that it was being led by his own sister.

'A white band can't play reggae,' he said. 'It's not right.'

'Thanks a bunch mate!' Danny was offended. As well he might be.

'I didn't mean you. I mean… I don't see you as…' He tailed off as Danny folded his arms and waited for him to dig himself so deep, he'd never get out.

'I think we should vote on it,' said Max, trying to defuse the situation.

'I don't know,' said Tyra. 'Maybe we should just leave it. Pete's right. It doesn't really fit in with the rest of our stuff.'

But Danny and Max took a rare stand and insisted on a vote. It was three votes to two. Brian, shockingly, voted for the song. Peter and Tyra against.

They played it as an encore at their next gig.

Much to Peter's disgust, the audience loved it.

Twenty-Three

Is it true that if we don't learn from history, we're doomed to repeat it?

Helen wrote this when she got back from lunch with Bridget that day. She kept a pretty, bound notebook by the side of her bed for those kinds of questions and observations. This one had a William Morris design on the cover. It had been a Christmas present from Elin, who had observed her mother's habit of collecting words. And it was already half full of fragments of things seen and remembered. Quotes that inspired her. And thoughts of her own. She wrote poems in her notebooks too. This one had three completed, and random lines of another. Though she never showed them to anyone.

Now, sitting in the armchair that looked out over dusk-faded rooftops, Helen went back to Kristina's death. She felt like a cold case detective sifting through evidence examined too many times and still not filed.

-0-0-0-

It was impossible to understand any of it without Kristina. Helen had always felt she was like a second mother to her. A glamorous, vibrant, warm mother, who she felt proud to be seen with. Her own mum, jealous of the influence Peter's family had on her, resented Kristina deeply. And there were times when comments like, 'I suppose you'll be spending the weekend with those lah di dah Alströms' threatened to make her mother's insecure fear of being supplanted into a self-fulfilling prophecy.

Kristina, who always went out of her way to ask about Helen's parents, was oblivious to the resentment in Rotherham. She imagined that Helen's mum would be relieved to know that her daughter had a caring family watching over her while she was living far away. She was very fond of Helen. She felt that she was a good influence on both her children. And they had a lot in common. They liked the same books and films and music. They loved to meet and have deep conversations. Their friendship had grown over the years, even as the early passion drained from Helen's relationship with Peter.

-0-0-0-

A few days before Kristina's death, the pair had met for lunch, as they often did in the school holidays.

They were in their favourite café in Soho. The place was scruffy, with wood panelled walls and bad paintings of the Bay of Naples. The ceiling fan was huge and creaky and wafted warm air and the smell of cooking cheese around the place. But the food was authentic. And Kristina was particularly fond of the Chianti, which was rich and red and served by the carafe.

She was worried about Tyra. 'She seems to be avoiding me,' she said, over her Caprese salad. 'Is she okay?'

Helen didn't know what to say. She was worried about Tyra too. She knew that she'd flunked her final year at Uni. Tyra had whispered it to her over instant Nescafé on the patio of the London house. 'Dad'll be furious!' she'd said glumly. 'And then he'll make life miserable for Mum. I know I'm going to have to tell them, but I keep chickening out.'

Helen remembered how embarrassed Tyra had been to confess her failure. It shouldn't have happened. She'd always been a straight-A student before. Though Helen guessed her grades must have been sliding for a while.

She felt angry with Peter about it. And she'd told him so. 'You've been putting too much pressure on her!' she'd said. 'How the hell could she concentrate on her studies when she's been juggling all those gigs and rehearsals. And she's wrecked half the time too… Are you still giving her tranquillisers? You promised me you'd stop that.'

He'd been defensive, as he always was when he was criticised. 'I don't know where she gets her drugs,' he'd replied. 'From the doctor probably, like me. Or from those dodgy gay friends of hers. Or both. And as far as the band goes, she always told me she enjoyed it. It's just stage fright with the singing. She's fine once she's up there. In fact, she's bloody good. And she can always say no if she really doesn't want to do it anymore.'

Helen was incensed at this. 'She says no all the time Peter! I've heard her asking you about getting another singer. You don't bloody listen to her. Sometimes I think you're just like your father.'

This was an insult too far for him. Particularly as it was true in this instance. They hadn't spoken for a week after that. But they'd drifted back together in the end. It was that kind of a relationship. More and more, Helen thought, she only stuck with it because she loved the two women in her boyfriend's life.

'I don't know,' she said, finally answering Kristina's question. 'I must admit, I wish Peter hadn't pressurised her into singing with the band. She hates it so much. He promised it was only temporary. But that was months ago. And he's got Brian to play keyboards since then. Now he knows how good she is, I really don't think he has any intention of finding anyone else.'

Kristina nodded gravely. 'She has a lovely voice,' she said. And for a horrible moment, Helen thought she might side with Peter. 'But she's always hated being in the limelight. I've never really understood why. But I guess it's just like that for some people. I'll have a word with Peter about it. Tyra has always hero-worshipped him, and he mustn't exploit that. It isn't fair.'

'Thank you!'

Their conversation drifted to other topics. Anecdotes about the kids at Helen's school. Isak's frustrations with his publisher. The leaking roof at Renton Hall.

They touched on Peter's latest dip into depression, and his new medication.

'So, he's on amitriptyline now?' Kristina clarified. 'Do you think it's helping him?'

Helen wasn't sure. 'It's early days,' she said, in the interests of diplomacy. Peter's depressions could be triggered by the smallest of setbacks. A bad gig. A song not well received by the band.... or the audience. People could wound him too easily. Max and Danny were more comfortable with each other than they would ever be with him. Of course they were. They'd grown up together. But it upset him, particularly when he was already feeling low. And he felt his lack of close male friends keenly.

'His father was always too hard on him,' Kristina said sadly, refilling her empty wine glass. She topped up Helen's too, while she was holding the carafe.

Helen wondered what to say.

Did you never think of leaving him? would have felt more like an accusation than a question, because she knew that Kristina adored her 'difficult' husband despite all his faults.

'But he always meant it for the best,' said Kristina, in the absence of a response.

Helen knew she was meant to agree with this, but she couldn't. Isak was a bully. He was hard on his son because it made him feel good. There was no altruism in it.

'And Tyra?' said Kristina, feeling the awkward silence between them and coming back to her concerns about her daughter. 'I'll talk to Peter about the singing. But do you think she's okay generally? She isn't having any relationship problems is she? I imagine she must have quite a few young men pursuing her?'

It was a reasonable question. Tyra had turned into a stunning young woman. But there was an edge of uncertainty in her mother's voice.

'Yes, I'm sure there must be,' said Helen. There were certainly men amongst the friends who sometimes turned up at the house with Tyra. Though Peter insisted they were all gay. 'But she's just a kid.'

'She's older than you and Peter were when you got together.'

Kristina smiled fondly at her as she said this. And Helen felt bad for the thought, 'I rest my case,' that flashed through her mind.

She was saved by the waiter bringing Tiramisu, the speciality of the house.

'This looks lovely. Thank you!'

Kristina waited until he had moved on to the next table, fishing his order-pad from the back pocket of his trousers. 'Anyway…. Promise me you won't tell anyone.' She looked at Helen with shining eyes. 'Arne Karlsson has contacted me. He wants me to tour with his band. I feel so rusty. But I must admit, I'd love to do it.'

Helen's first thought was of Isak, as Kristina's must have been.

'That's wonderful,' she said, trying to push dark thoughts of the man out of her mind. 'When?'

'This autumn.'

'Wow! How's Mr Alström taken the news?' She never had been able to bring herself to call him Isak, and Kristina had long since given up trying to persuade her to.

Across the table, those brilliant blue eyes clouded. 'I haven't told him yet,' she said. 'He never wanted me to work, you see. But now the children are grown up. And Peter, at least, is in good hands…'

Helen smiled at that, gratified at the compliment.

'And Isak's away so often with his book tours and speaking engagements. I get quite lonely on my own at Renton Hall.'

'I'm sure he'll be pleased for you.'

Helen had wondered many times why she would say such a thing. Had she wanted so much for Kristina to be happy, that she was prepared to ignore the truth? Tyra wouldn't have said it. Or Peter. They'd have tried harder to protect their mother. Sometimes she attempted to console herself by thinking that Kristina had chosen to confide in her rather than in either of her children because she wanted, just for a few more days, to hold on to the dream.

'I have to make a decision by the 14th,' she'd said, with a slight quiver in her voice. 'I'll need to discuss it with him before that.'

She glanced at her watch then. As if the mere thought of telling her husband had made her nervous of not being at home when he got back.

'Speaking of which, I'd better not miss my train. Time goes so quickly when we meet. But I think we've just got time for a cappuccino? And this is on me, sweetheart. I insist. I'm grateful to you for sacrificing a day of your precious holiday to meet up with your boyfriend's elderly mother!'

They'd both laughed at that. And Kristina had hailed the waiter again to order coffee and the bill.

They'd parted at Leicester Square tube station with hugs and promises to meet again very soon.

Less than a fortnight later, Kristina was dead.

Helen's eyes filled with tears as she remembered the gentleness of the woman who never did become her mother-in-law. She remembered how Kristina had always seen the best in Isak. Always excused the worst. She wondered, if she'd broken her promise that day and told Peter, or Tyra…. Maybe they would have intervened in some way. And maybe Kristina would not have died that fateful night.

-0-0-0-

The August of 1975 was hot. By 10am on the 10th, she'd felt the temperature already edging towards the high twenties.

It was a Sunday and she'd stayed over at Peter's. No-one else in the house was likely to emerge much before lunchtime. And she had the luxury of the kitchen to herself. She made a mug of coffee, ignoring, for once, the unwashed pots in the sink and the smelliness of the pedal bin, and headed outside with a folding chair to the small, paved area at the back of the house.

She felt tired and heavy. And she had a strange inexplicable feeling of dread.

It was the kind of feeling she'd always had as a child when a thunderstorm was on the way. And she scanned the clear blue sky for any sign of dark clouds approaching. But there was nothing.

She thought that she should have been feeling good. It was the school holidays, after all.

And Alstrom had had a great gig last night. A wild afterparty too by the sound of the merriment that had continued into the early hours.

Finally, it seemed the band were building a following.

She'd started to recognise some of the same people turning up at their gigs. With a singer capable of holding a tune, Peter was writing more vocal-heavy songs. He'd also allowed 'Stonewall is Coming', a new song by Tyra, into their setlist, ganging up with his sister and Brian to outvote Max and Danny this time, on the grounds that he didn't care if their masculinity felt threatened by it.

Helen wondered at the time if he'd done that out of revenge for their mutiny over 'Madhouse Reggae'. But she was glad anyway. She liked the song. And with Patti Smith's Horses still just a twinkle in Arista's eye, there was precious little else going on for a gay audience in the summer of '75.

She'd gone to bed around 1am. Never a heavy drinker, and without the adrenalin rush of a performance to burn off, she invariably felt tired just as the Alstrom parties were getting started.

Peter hated her bowing out early. But he'd come to expect it. That night he'd been stoned and boring the pants off Bridget, who'd shown more interest recently in coming to Alstrom gigs. They were all getting off their heads to 'Pictures at An Exhibition'. Always Helen's cue to head for bed.

She'd finally drifted to sleep halfway through 'The Great Gates of Kiev'. Peter had climbed in beside her at about 3am. But his antidepressants (or the depression underneath them) had muted his never very high sex drive, so it had been easy enough to pretend that he hadn't woken her up.

And now it was the morning after the night before for all of them. And she was the only one capable of greeting the day. She hugged her coffee mug and stared across at the buildings opposite. There were some offices, deserted on a Sunday. Most of the bigger houses had been converted into apartments, and most of the windows had curtains still drawn. A woman pegging bedclothes onto a washing line; probably in breach of the archaic byelaws, was the only visible sign of life. Though the smell of Full English breakfast suggested that the café on the corner was open.

That traditional Sunday morning smell made Helen realise that she was hungry. And she was wondering whether the party-people would have left any bread untoasted as the night progressed and the munchies set in.

But then the phone rang.

This was unusual. Most of the band's friends would know that they wouldn't be up yet, even on a normal Sunday.

She felt irritated at her peace being disturbed, and wandered into the hallway to answer it, half hoping it would stop ringing before she got there.

It didn't.

'Hello?' she said.

'Is Tyra there?' It was Isak, and he sounded weird, shaken.

'Oh, Hi Mr Alström. It's Helen. She's still in bed, I'm afraid. Can I take a message for her?'

'No. Get her out of bed please. I need to speak to her.'

'Is everything ok?' The dread she'd felt earlier seemed to amplify, tightening around her throat.

'No... Please, just get Tyra for me, will you?'

'Ok, yes, of course!'

She took the stairs two at a time and knocked on Tyra's door.

There was a long pause before it opened. Bridget peered out. She was wearing Tyra's dressing gown, pulled on hastily.

She clutched the front together in an attempt at modesty. For a couple of beats, Helen didn't understand what was going on. And then she did.

'I'm sorry!' said her friend. 'This is really embarrassing…'

Helen felt a flash of anger, though she didn't know why. She tried to swallow it down, but it seemed to stick in her throat. And when she spoke, her voice sounded strangled.

'Can you get Tyra please? It's urgent. Her dad's on the phone.'

Bridget's eyes widened slightly. 'Oh God!' she said. 'I hope her mum's okay.'

Helen stood outside, impatiently, hearing Bridget's soft voice within, murmuring, 'Tyra, sweetheart. Come on, get up. Your dad's on the phone.'

Bridget's exclamation had crystalized Helen's fears. She remembered her conversation with Kristina. And she felt engulfed with the terror of it.

When Tyra emerged, she was in T-shirt and pants..

She ran barefoot, downstairs to the hallway, rubbing her eyes, and picked up the phone.

Bridget stood beside Helen. They both held their breath.

'Hello… Dad?'

There was a long pause. Then Tyra sank to the floor of the hallway, her back against the wall. 'Yes,' she said faintly. 'Of course. Yes. I'll tell Peter. I'll be with you…. What time is it now..? As soon as possible…. Will you be okay? Are you sure? Okay. Yes. Bye.'

She was still staring at the phone when Helen reached her in the hallway.

She looked stunned. And dry eyed.

'Mum's dead,' she said. 'There was an accident last night… in the car. God, I've got to tell Peter. How the hell am I going to do that?'

-0-0-0-

Peter howled in disbelief, clinging to his sister, and sobbing into her as a child might sob into a pet dog or teddy bear. His wailing sent shudders down Helen's spine and brought tears smarting into her own eyes. He was inconsolable, and in denial. 'Maybe it's not true,' he said finally, clutching at some glimmer of hope in his desolation. 'It's the kind of thing Dad might say as a joke you know.'

At the time, Helen had thought that must be an exaggeration. There was no doubt that Isak could be cruel, but surely even he would have baulked at this.

She discovered later that it was exactly the kind of sick 'joke' he had played on his son back in the distant days of his childhood.

But Tyra knew her father's games. And she knew this wasn't one of them.

'No,' she said. 'I think it's true.'

Helen hovered in the doorway, feeling useless, noticing that it was his sister that Peter was clinging to, and not her. She felt stiff, and uncomfortable and didn't know what to do. So she stood there, silently, wishing she could just leave them to it, watching and waiting for something to relieve the tension.

'I said I'd go home,' said Tyra, gently to her still sobbing brother. 'I don't think there's anything much I can do. But I guess Dad needs me. Will you come, or do you prefer to stay here with Helen?'

'I want to come with you.' He tightened his grip on her. Helen could see his fingers digging into her back through the thin T-shirt. She thought he must be bruising her.

But it was as if he were afraid that she may be snatched from him too.

Tyra glanced uncomfortably round at Helen. 'Do you think you could pack him an overnight bag?' she asked.

'Sure!' Helen was relieved to have something to do.

An hour later, she waved them off in Peter's car.

She was aware of Bridget, dressed now, hovering behind her in the hallway. Max and Danny, realising that some Alström tragedy was unfolding, were keeping well out of the way in their rooms with whichever girls they'd bedded for the night. Brian, of course, had left the party early and would be playing the organ now at his local Methodist church before going home for Sunday roast with his mum.

'God! I'm so sorry!' said Bridget. 'I know how much you loved her.'

Loneliness swept over Helen. At the loss of Kristina. And her exclusion from the all-consuming grief of the two Alström siblings.

'She was like a mother to me,' she stammered, trying to find words to express her grief.

'I know love, I know. Come here!'

She turned bleakly and allowed herself to be enfolded in Bridget's arms.

-0-0-0-

After Kristina's funeral, the family went back to Renton Hall. It was September 1975. And after the long hot days of summer, the edges of the leaves were turning red and gold.

For Helen, this was the first time she had returned there since Kristina's death. The old house felt like the heart had been ripped from it.

Standing miserably in the hallway with Peter and Tyra beneath the brooding portrait of Isak, she thought they must have looked like three lost orphans, delivered to a grand house for reasons unknown.

Isak was putting his beloved Bentley in the garage.

They hadn't wanted to leave him there alone that night. But they didn't want to be there either.

Memories of her first Alström Christmas haunted Helen. The tree, smelling of the forest with its lights and strings of tiny Swedish flags. The gnomes and the straw goats. The candles over the fireplace. And the carols. Kristina's beautiful, smoky voice mingling with the music of her children.

'I'm going to bed!' said Isak, barely looking at them as he turned the key in the large oak door and headed towards the staircase that led towards the master bedroom.

His face seemed dark with anger or pain, or maybe grief. He made no effort to comfort or console his children.

They watched his slow progress up the stairs. His feet landing heavily on the worn treads. His hand clutching the bannister. It felt disrespectful to turn their backs before he was out of sight.

But then silently, Tyra led them down the hallway. They took the narrow staircase that the servants would have used in days gone by. And headed for their own rooms.

-0-0-0-

An hour later, showered and in her dressing gown, Helen saw Tyra on her way to the bathroom.

She had stripped out of her funeral clothes and wore a baggy T-shirt and pyjama bottoms.

Helen tried not to notice the soft contours of her breasts through the thin cotton. Or the way her smooth arms were tanned from long idle afternoons lying on the back patio at home. Or how her feet were bare, and also golden brown.

She tried to ignore the pounding of her heart as Tyra came towards her in the narrow corridor with its uneven, creaking floorboards.

She swallowed anxiously, and stepped back, realising that she did this more and more, and hoping that Tyra didn't notice and think she was the kind of straight girl who was frightened of being 'hit on' by lesbians.

If she thought that, she never showed it.

'I think you should be with Peter,' she whispered. 'He shouldn't be on his own tonight.'

It was exactly what her mother would have said.

Though Helen realised instantly that it wasn't what she'd wanted to hear.

'You're sure your dad won't object?'

'I don't really care, to be honest.'

At some point between the death of Kristina and the

funeral, Tyra had told her father that she had failed her degree. In the past, he would have excused her. But he'd sensed that she'd been avoiding him. And her academic failure was a convenient hook to hang his hurt feelings upon. All day, Helen had felt the chilliness that hung now in the air between the Master of the House and his golden girl.

Helen crept to Peter's room and pushed open the creaking door.

He was in his old boyhood single bed. The curtains were open, and moonlight bathed the room. Two huge Roger Dean posters graced the walls. One beside his wardrobe, and another opposite. A model biplane was suspended by a string from the ceiling, moving slightly in the breeze from the open window.

She couldn't tell if Peter was asleep. She wondered if he was pretending. But he was swaddled tightly in his bedclothes with only the halo of his hair showing above them.

She whispered his name, just in case, but he didn't stir.

Softly, she backed from his room and returned to her own, remembering Kristina making sure she would be comfortable there that first Christmas, not quite five years ago. From there, her thoughts jumped to their last meeting. The final hug goodbye at Leicester Square. Wreathed in smiles. Their promise to meet again soon. A promise that would never now be kept.

She didn't want to be in there, alone, with her memories. The ghosts of Renton Hall seemed closer now without Kristina.

At the end of the corridor, she heard Tyra leaving the bathroom, switching out the light, returning to her room.

She lasted, maybe, ten minutes before she followed her, closing the door of her own room behind her, hesitating for just a moment before knocking.

-0-0-0-

There was a long pause before Tyra came to the door. But Helen didn't think she'd been planning on going to bed. She could see the counterpane unruffled in the soft light of the bedside lamp.

And she could see that Tyra had been crying.

She'd mopped away the tears from her cheeks, but her eyes still brimmed with them.

She looked dazed, and Helen couldn't tell from her expression whether she was pleased to see her or not.

'Is Peter okay?' she asked.

'He's fine. He's asleep.'

Tyra nodded, and relaxed visibly. 'He'll have taken something,' she said, as if that were a good thing.

Helen thought that Tyra had probably 'taken something' too.

'I thought I'd just see how you are,' she said.

Tyra looked surprised. 'I'm okay,' she said.

Helen didn't think so, but she knew Tyra well enough to know that she'd never get the truth about that. She thought of the funeral that afternoon. The packed church. People openly weeping as they placed flowers on the coffin. Peter with his long blonde hair tumbling over the shoulders of his black suit, sobbing. Isak, stony-faced, white-tied, so obviously loathed by Kristina's family, rumbling out the eulogy and drawing sympathy from his English friends for his stoic grief. And Tyra, in that distant world she seemed to have inhabited ever since her mother's death, locked away from them all.

'I wondered if I could just sit with you for a while,' said Helen.

'Yes, of course.'

That damned politeness again. Shutting everything in. And everyone out.

Tyra gestured her into the room. Unlike Peter's, which had been updated, at least in its artwork, it seemed frozen in late adolescence. There was a purple bedspread. And lavender walls. She had Jimi Hendrix album sleeves mounted on the wall behind her bed. A record deck, tuner and speakers were stacked beside the dressing table, which had a dusty collection of gonks and trolls and a school photograph in a silver frame.

'I'm sorry about the décor,' she said. 'I thought it was pretty cool when I was sixteen. But now it just gives me a headache.'

Helen could see what she meant.

'My bedroom at home's still pink,' she said, trying to level the playing field of embarrassment a little. 'Dad painted it for me when I was eleven and I've never been able to bring myself to ask if I could change it.'

'I bet you've got a fluffy bunny pyjama case too,' said Tyra, teasing her a little.

'How did you guess….? Do you think anyone, ever actually kept their pyjamas in those things?'

They both laughed gently at the absurdity of pyjama cases. And Tyra's discomfort seemed to ease a little.

'I was just sitting in the window seat, looking out,' she said. 'It's nice there. Though, window seat is a bit of a grand term for it. It's really just a blanket box with cushions on it.'

But it felt so right to have it there, as if people would have chosen to sit there for centuries. It looked out over the driveway, the lawns and the orchards to the trees and the wall that was Renton's boundary with the rest of the world.

She sat down there again, and Helen followed her, pushing herself into the left hand corner of the seat opposite Tyra.

As Helen sat, she wondered how many wives and daughters had watched and waited, for suitors, for friends, for sons to return from wars. And she thought too of husbands shut out from the labour of childbirth. And of illicit lovers waiting for the hours when the rest of the household slept.

She felt aroused by the closeness of Tyra and the thought of illicit love. It felt terrible to experience such a thing on such a day. She forced herself to breathe.

Through the leaded window she could see the silhouettes of trees, still clinging to their turning leaves, an indigo sky dotted with stars, and a moon reclining lazily like a painting in a book of nursery rhymes.

Beside her, she saw Tyra, her face pale and drawn, her stunning blue eyes red-rimmed, her inky hair, as wavy as her brother's, but dark, like coal. She looked as if she were waiting for Helen to say something.

And Helen felt compelled to obey.

'How did you get to be so self-sufficient?' she asked, wonderingly.

Tyra shrugged. 'Is that how I come across? I don't feel it....

Never, really, but especially not now. Not without Mum.' Her voice trembled.

Helen wanted to hold her. But she didn't dare.

Tyra seemed still to be trying to make sense of what Helen had asked her. 'I suppose I had to learn to look like I was okay when I was at boarding school. It could be rough there if you were a cry baby.'

'God, what went wrong with Peter then?' Helen bit her lip, regretting the disloyalty as soon as the words were out of her mouth.

Tyra glanced at her, and she didn't look surprised. 'Things really aren't all that great with you two, are they?' she asked.

Helen wondered if she should try to paper over her mistake. Laugh it off maybe. But she felt like if she did that now, when someone had asked her directly, she'd be trapped into doing it for the rest of her life.

'Well… of course… this wouldn't be a great time for anyone,' she began cautiously.

'No, that's true! But you weren't happy, even before Mum died. She didn't want to see it, of course. She loved you to bits and she was always so keen to have you as a daughter-in-law. I imagine Peter doesn't seem quite so much like husband material without her though.'

Helen searched Tyra's face for some clue to how she felt about that. But she wasn't giving anything away.

'Pete's had a rough time,' Tyra continued. 'To answer your question. Dad's always been awful to him. Do you remember when he thought the news about Mum could be one of Dad's 'jokes'? Well, that happened. Dad took him on a camping holiday when he was about nine years old. He always wanted to toughen Pete up. But Peter has never been a tough guy. He was homesick. He hated all that 'macho stuff'…. Nude swimming in the lake and chopping wood and digging firepits. He wanted to be at home, with his music and model airplanes. Dad got frustrated with him. So he told him he'd brought him away to break the news that Mum was dead. Peter had no way of knowing the truth. Dad had picked him up from school to go on the trip. He sobbed his heart out for two days before Dad finally admitted it was 'just a joke'. That kind of thing doesn't make people stronger. It destroys them.'

Helen was horrified. She pictured the nine year old Peter she'd seen in photographs. Just a kid. How distraught he would have been. 'I had no idea!' she said. 'I've seen how critical he is of Peter…. But that's just… sadistic.'

Tyra laughed bitterly. 'You haven't seen even so much as a fraction of it. Mum never did either. I'm sure I don't even know the full extent of it either, because Peter won't… or probably, more accurately… can't, talk about it.'

Helen shook her head, trying to take this in. Her parents were stiff and undemonstrative. Her mother could be cutting at times. Particularly in recent years since Helen had seemed to prefer being with Peter's family. On occasion, during her growing up, both her parents had hurt Helen's feelings, wounded her unintentionally, not been there for her when she'd needed them. But they never would have deliberately chosen to hurt her… Never.

'But Peter still loves him!' she said, puzzled.

Tyra shrugged. 'Of course!' she said. 'Don't we all love our parents, even when we hate them?'

Helen had no answer to that. It was a theory she'd never needed to test. Though, she found her thoughts going to some of the teenagers at school and how loyal they could be to the parents who abused them.

There was a long silence before she changed the subject. 'Do you think you and Bridget will become an item?' It was a question that had haunted her since that awful Sunday morning when they all first heard the news. The idea consumed her with jealousy. And shame.

'No, it's too hard, thinking I was with her while Mum was dying.'

Her voice shook as she said this, and Helen wished she hadn't asked.

She put her hand over Tyra's on the cushion and was surprised at how warm it was. She tucked her fingers underneath, wanting to share in that heat.

There was an answering movement, and Helen looked up, shocked, into her eyes.

It was like drowning in blue.

The dark mirror of the window reflected their move towards each other. She lost focus, telling herself that one kiss never hurt anyone. That old perennial lie.

Tyra's lips were soft. There the taste of salt upon them. And heat flooded through Helen, as if she had been frozen for the longest of times and never known it.

She pulled away, searching Tyra's face for reassurance.

And Tyra, who had loved this woman for years, half-cut, and numbed out on grief, pulled her gently back. She cupped Helen's face in her hands and kissed her again.

-0-0-0-

They barely heard the tapping on the door at first. They were too lost in each other.

But then the tapping came again, accompanied this time by Peter's voice whispering 'Ty...'

And the two women sprang apart, instinctively smoothing themselves down as Tyra muttered 'Shit!' under her breath and bounded across the room.

'Pete!' she said, opening the door, just enough to peep out and give Helen more chance to compose herself. 'Are you ok love?'

'I dreamt that Mum had come home,' he sobbed.

'Oh... sweetheart!' Tyra stepped out of the room and pulled the door closed behind her.

Helen sat helplessly in the window seat. She knew that Peter must have walked past her door to reach his sister's. She listened to his strangled sobs. And Tyra's gentle, murmured words of comfort.

She thought that Tyra would eventually walk him back to his room. She wasn't prepared for what happened next, as the door opened again and she heard Tyra saying, 'I bet you were looking for Helen, weren't you? Well she had been to see if you were okay. But you were asleep. So she'd just popped by to check in on me.'

Helen thought she might die of embarrassment as she saw her boyfriend revealed by the opening door.

He looked wretchedly between the two remaining women in his life. And Helen knew without a doubt that he hadn't been looking for her that night, any more than he had reached for her on the Sunday of Kristina's death.

She forced herself to smile and step forward as Tyra handed her to him.

Twenty-Four

WEDNESDAY 10TH APRIL 2019

Peter was finding it no easy feat, putting his 'affairs' in order. And his decision to do it quietly, secretly, made it harder.

If James Hargreave, his solicitor, had concerns, he didn't show it. James' father, Simeon, had looked after the Alström family's legalities for almost forty years. Their file was many inches thick. Simeon, knowing the history, would have been wondering about Peter's state of mind. He would have asked him more about how he was. And what had led him to make these big decisions.

But James didn't care about any of that. As far as he was concerned, Peter Alström was just another client who could do whatever he wanted with his money so long as it was legal. James was as sharp as his grey Savile Row suit. And all he was really bothered about was accumulating enough billable hours to retire to the Bahamas while he was still young enough to enjoy them.

When Peter had finished telling James what he wanted, the solicitor stood up at the far side of the impossibly large conference table where he conducted his business. He smoothed his tie.

'I'll put this in writing and send you a copy to read over and sign,' he said.

Peter struggled to his feet. 'Well… thank you,' he said, a little shocked by the speed with which he was being dismissed.

The room was bland, with just the huge table, a painting of coloured rectangles on the wall, and a large window looking out onto the street, where it was starting to rain.

'How long…?'

'Just a couple of days,' said James, quickly. 'I'll get my secretary to type it up now.'

'Ok, thank you!'

The receptionist, Maureen, watched Peter sympathetically as he emerged from the office. She remembered him from Simeon's days. In her youth she'd thought he was 'dishy'. She'd barely recognised him a couple of weeks earlier when he'd come to speak to James about his father's Will.

'It's raining quite heavily outside,' she said. 'We have some umbrellas beside the door if you'd like to borrow one.'

Peter glanced up confused. He felt disorientated, like when he was a small child and his father used to physically pick him up and hurl him into the air for fun.

'Thank you,' he said. 'But I'll be ok. My car's parked just outside.'

'Ok,' said Maureen. 'Have a nice day!' Then she kicked

herself for insensitivity, remembering that he'd just lost his father.

-0-0-0-

Alstrom were on the tea break of their final rehearsal before Holy Week.

Tyra located Max and Danny shrouded in their own microclimate of smog, perched outside on a wall by the church lychgate.

She handed them a mug each as Danny's phone rang.

'Yeah!' he bellowed into it. 'What?... Can't hear you love... Hang on...'

'There's a good signal over by the church,' said Max helpfully.

'Right mate. Cheers!' He scampered off in search of better reception.

'New bird!' said Max, with a bemused shrug. 'I think he's smitten.'

'Really?'

'Yeah... I know... I was surprised too. He met her at the studio apparently. She's in a tribute band. 'Fleetwood Mackerel'. Nice looking! Not bad at all for her age. Where's Elin, by the way?'

'Talking to her beloved on the phone.'

'It's just you and me for the Lonely Hearts Tea Club then.'

'I'm afraid so!'

Max dragged on his cigarette. A genuine Marlborough, not one of Danny's 'specials'.

'How do you think it's going?'

Tyra thought about this. 'I think it's heading in the right direction,' she said.

Max shrugged. 'I'm sure it'll be alright on the night. It usually is. It's just a shame we've got this interruption now, but there's no way I can be taking any time out this week. The Bishop's already threatened to throw my nuts in the fire.'

'How come? I thought we'd been immaculately well behaved.'

'Me too! But that grovelling rat of a church warden told him he'd found a groupie in one of the meeting rooms.'

Tyra spluttered into laughter at this.

'Seriously?'

'I know! The man's such a chuffin' drama queen. And he hates my guts. I told the Bish it was probably one of the Salsa dancers who'd got lost looking for the loos. But he wasn't having any of it.'

Tyra studied him intently. 'You really care about this job, don't you?'

'Yes...of course I do!'

'You know, I never had you down as a spiritual kind of a person.'

'Well, you know... it's not an easy thing to admit when you're in your twenties. You think people are gonna laugh.'

'I wouldn't have laughed!'

'No, well you're different. Didn't Elin track you down in some convent in Spain?'

'It was a Buddhist Retreat Centre.'

'Well, there you go then!' He stubbed out the cigarette and blew on his tea.

'So, do you believe in it?' Tyra asked. 'God… I mean… And all that stuff.'

She'd noticed that it didn't always seem to be a requirement of the job.

'Yeah… I do… in my own way.'

'What happened? Did you have a Road to Damascus conversion or something?'

'No, I started going to a Church Youth Club when I was a kid. I played in their band and just kind of got into it from there. I fancied being a monk at one point, but then the obvious got in the way.'

'Wow! Max. You kept that very well hidden.'

'Yeah. Well, not anymore. How about you, Mrs 'Road to Enlightenment'? Do you believe in all that Buddhist stuff?'

'I don't know! Ask me in twenty more years. If I'm still alive!' She looked through the gate to the headstones of the graves beyond. All those people whose lives had seemed so crucial to so many people, now barely remembered. So many of those final resting places untended, but still peaceful under the grey Essex sky. By the church doorway, Danny was pacing, talking animatedly into his phone. He looked happy.

'That's sweet,' she said. 'About Danny.'

'Yeah! So, what's the latest with you and Helen? Have you two managed to hook up again yet?'

Tyra was shocked out of her reverie. 'I'm sorry?'

'Oh, come on Ty, don't give me that innocent look. Even Peter would have seen it if he hadn't had his head quite so far up his own backside.'

'I didn't realise we were so obvious!'

'No... well, sorry to disillusion you and all that. But have you seen her yet?'

'No!'

'Spoken to her, at least?'

'No.'

'For goodness sake. You blithering wuss. Did I teach you nothing? Go see her. Take chocolate, it never fails. You've got a perfect excuse with Easter Sunday next week. It's the most erotic food known to man. Melts at body temperature. Much better than flowers! God, I had some fun with chocolate buttons back in the day!'

He finished his tea and beckoned to Danny. 'Come on then. Let's get back to the grindstone. I just found out that the singer with 'Rats in the Stairwell' is the Vicar of St Swithin's son. And I'm damned if I'm going to make a total dick of myself in front of the opposition.'

-0-0-0-

Later, as they were packing up, Elin asked Max if she could speak to him in private.

Tyra figured she should make herself scarce.

'Meet you outside by the car!' she called, slinging the laptop case onto her shoulder. 'See you Monday week Max. Have a Good Easter.'

Danny, who, with his loanable equipment and van, had become the band's designated roadie, hauled a trolley-load of kit out of the hall after her.

And Elin and Max were left alone.

Elin shuffled uncomfortably. But she needn't have worried. Max had morphed seamlessly into vicar mode. 'I'm assuming that lucky young man of yours has popped the question,' he said, ever the romantic.

Elin looked startled. 'No... Well, actually he did, a few weeks back, but I thought he was joking so I said 'no'.'

'Oh!' Max looked disappointed. 'So, you're not asking me to marry you... as it were?'

'No! Though, of course, if we ever did decide to tie the knot, we'd want you to do it.'

'Oh, well that's good. And I'd be extremely honoured... So, what can I do for you?'

Elin was still surprised at the change in her bandmate. He looked and sounded every inch the kindly vicar. She was impressed.

'This is confidential, isn't it?'

'Is it a confession?' Max asked, startled.

'Yes, I guess it might be.'

'Then yes. It's confidential.'

Elin's eyes brimmed with tears of relief.

Max led her gently to one of the chairs at the side of the hall.

She sat, and he sat beside her, quietly, waiting.

'I think Dad had something to do with Grandad's death,' she said. Then she buried her face in her hands and began to sob.

-0-0-0-

'Oh!' said Max. 'That's taken me by surprise rather!'

He dug a handful of clean tissues out of his jacket pocket and handed them to her.

'But, seriously, you won't have to tell anybody, will you?'

'No... I promise I won't tell anyone. But your grandad died of a stroke. And I can't see how that could have anything to do with your dad... What makes you suspect this?'

Elin blew her nose noisily and mopped at her eyes. She'd surprised herself with the force of her outburst, and now she felt shaky and disorientated.

Slowly she gathered herself as Max glanced anxiously towards the door. He was cursing himself for not taking the girl somewhere more private. He hoped that no-one would wander into the hall at this vital moment. Particularly the Church Warden, who was bound to misconstrue it.

'I saw a piece in the local press,' she stammered, through chattering teeth. 'I'm sorry, I've been sitting on this for days.'

'You haven't spoken to Dave then? Or your mum?'

'No, I wanted to talk to someone who wouldn't jump to any ideas about what I should do. I need to figure that out for myself.'

'Good plan. So... you were saying?'

'I saw an article about Grandad's funeral in the local rag. And it said that Dad found Grandad at 7.30. But the thing is, Dad was there at twenty to five. Look...'

She showed Max the text. His heart sank as he looked at it.

'It's probably a typo in the paper,' he said.

'They're usually pretty careful about stuff like that.'

Max handed the phone back. 'I'm sure there's a logical explanation,' he said soothingly.

'But what if they'd had a fight or something?'

Max scanned back over the years he'd spent with Peter. Was he capable of this? He didn't truly know.

'I don't think so,' he said. 'Look, why don't you have a word with him? Honestly, I'm sure there will be a perfectly logical explanation.' Or, at least, he thought, an opportunity for Peter to calm his daughter's fears with a plausible lie.

'I don't want him to think that I would imagine such a terrible thing if it isn't true.'

Max understood this. He also found that uncomfortable thoughts were intruding now. Memories of Peter's complaints about his father. Of his sudden flare of temper once when Max had tried to reason with him about Tyra. And of his behaviour recently, since his father died. Like a man bowed down with, maybe... not so much grief... as guilt.

'Let me think about this,' he said. He almost added 'And pray,' but he didn't think Elin seemed like a religious person and he didn't want to frighten her.

'And if you don't want to talk to your dad, maybe you could talk to Dave, or your mum... or even Tyra. You never know, they may have a perspective on this that neither of us could have thought of.'

'Okay,' she stood, uncertainly. 'I guess I'd better get going. Auntie Tyra will be getting cold out there.'

Max stood too. 'If you need to talk again. Anytime. Day or night,' he said. 'Just phone me.'

She flung her arms around him. 'You know, you're nowhere near as much of an idiot as you make yourself out to be.'

He smiled. 'Oh, trust me,' he said. 'Anyone can be an idiot. If they set their mind to it!'

Twenty-Five

Max was troubled by Elin's words.

They played on his mind that evening, tugging at his concentration as he attempted to think of something apposite to say in his Palm Sunday sermon. It was a busy evening too, with a lot of interruptions. He'd intervened by phone in what had threatened to become a full-scale punch up over the Easter Sunday flowers. And now he was flicking, with an unusual degree of apathy, through the profiles of an Over-Fifties Dating App, where he was careful to disguise his identity for fear of horrifying his Parishioners.

If he were to be completely honest, Max had always thought that Peter was a spoilt upper class drip. Sure, he'd had a rough time from his father. And that posh boarding school he went to had probably been a bit of a hell hole. But Max hadn't had it easy either, growing up on a rough estate in Dagenham with a depressed mum and a dad who spent most of his spare time (and cash) at the bookies. And Danny's background had been even harder, growing up a couple of streets away from Max, without any dad at all.

Max (real name Ken Maxwell) had learnt early on that it

was a dog eat dog world, and you had to be tough to survive it. He learnt how to be a joker to cover his insecurities. He developed the skill of chatting up every girl he met to hide his fear that no woman would ever love him. He discovered that the church youth club provided the only warm alternative to the street corner. And that beating the hell out of a battered drum kit was a good substitute for smashing his father's face in.

Danny, his lifelong best friend, with his gentler, laid back nature, was always going to be a natural for the bass. He was probably born to be a stoner too. Most likely, he got a taste for the stuff from his mother, while he was still chilling in the womb.

Max believed that the church and the Reverend Alan Bradwell had saved him. 'The Rev' as the kids always called him, had gone into the ministry fresh from the Second World War. He was tough, and he understood that you didn't have to have come under enemy fire to be traumatised. He'd had a rough time of it himself. He never said much, but Max knew that he understood about alcoholic dads, and mums who struggled to get out of bed on a morning.

Since Max had applied for the ministry, he'd striven to be a vicar like Alan. The old man was still his spiritual advisor. He seemed, at 96, to burn brighter than he ever had. But Max didn't want to burden him with this. He felt too embroiled somehow. Too guilty of something within it.

He knew he'd used Peter, back in the old days. He'd given plenty back too, of course. He was a damn good drummer. And he'd been a loyal foot soldier for Alstrom. But Peter had been his meal ticket out of monotony. Max knew how his life would have gone without the band. He'd already started work in the car factory at sixteen. He'd known that he'd have got some girl pregnant and be married at twenty. And then there'd have been the kids, and the grandkids and retirement. He'd always wanted more than that. But he'd been too lazy to join the army.

And then he saw Peter's advert. He showed it to Dan. They auditioned. Along with Susan, who tagged on everywhere with Danny back then. On the way home on the bus, the two lads had looked at each other and they hadn't needed to say anything. They both knew that Peter was a dreamer. They knew that he had about as much chance of success as the band they used to play in at the youth club. But he was a dreamer with money and connections. They could ditch their awful day jobs and play full time for him. And he had a bloody big house, with rooms to live in rent free. Peter had other people to see. He was going to get back to them in 'a day or two'. They both knew that would feel like the longest couple of days in the whole of their young lives. It looked like Susan might have been thinking the same. Though she enjoyed her job at the hairdressers more. But Susan wasn't looking at them. She'd rubbed a circle in the steamed up window of the bus, and she was staring dreamily out of it. Danny was always clueless about the ways of women. Max reckoned that's why he'd got himself lumbered with Susan so young. But Max understood what was going on with his best friend's girl. She thought she'd seen upgrade material in Peter, and she was already planning how to get into the pretty little rich boy's kecks.

Peter chose them of course. It was what the kids nowadays would call a 'no brainer'.

Max had fallen easily into the same jokey, superficial, back slapping approach to his new 'boss' that he'd used with his old one on the assembly line. But he'd never really taken to him. To Max, Peter seemed blessed beyond measure. He had bags of money and contacts through his mum to get them gigs all over the place. He was okay on guitar and violin. He wrote some decent songs. They were a bit flowery sometimes for Max's taste. But they were good enough if you liked that sort of thing. And Peter's girlfriend was hot. Not in an obvious, tarty way like Susan. But in the way of girls who don't know that they're hot at all. Quiet and unassuming and bloody beautiful.

Max felt sorry for Helen. And he figured she must have been truly besotted with Peter once to end up lumbered with him like that. It made him sick to see how she soothed her boyfriend's ego, stroked him, physically and mentally. Calmed him down when he was being a total dick. Peter could freak out about something that didn't matter at all. Like there being no light bulbs in the dressing room, or a gig getting cancelled at the last minute. Even somebody heckling them from the audience could send him into a tailspin. Eventually, even Helen started looking weary of it all. Work was hard for her and Peter was tiresome. Max remembered thinking it was like seeing something die before his eyes.

He'd fantasised a lot about what it would be like to console Helen when she finally realised that she'd backed a loser. But he'd always known there would be too many ramifications for it to ever happen. Life was too cushy with Peter to throw it away for some girl.

He wouldn't have wanted to upset Tyra either. He'd seen straight away that she was in love with Helen. He felt sorry for the kid. It seemed to him, at first, that she didn't have a chance in hell. In his book, back then, girls like Helen just weren't gay. But then he'd started to wonder. He started to notice little tell-tale signs that he'd learnt from dating books. The kind of signs that told him when he was 'in'. Daft little things like the way Helen's eyes went all soft when she looked at Tyra. And the way she blushed sometimes when she talked to her and cast little surreptitious glances in her direction whenever she was in the room. He couldn't say he blamed her. Tyra was pretty damn hot too, though a bit too boyish for his tastes. And she was nothing like her brother in temperament. She never expected special treatment. He was glad when Peter's old keyboard player left, and she started playing with the band. She fitted in and she worked hard. And she knew her place in the hierarchy well enough at first. Like Brian. But cooler. Poor old Brian could never be described as 'cool' in a million years. He wore hand knitted jumpers and had a naff haircut. He never touched drugs or alcohol. He followed Peter around like a lap dog. And he didn't live at the house with the rest of the band. He preferred to stay at home with his dear old mum.

Max swung his long legs up onto the sofa and stared at the ceiling, distracted, momentarily, by how he needed to dust the old fashioned light fitting. There were cobwebs up there, waving from the wings of the chubby-cheeked brass cherubs.

He hoped there weren't any spiders. They'd always given him the creeps.

Still, the million-dollar question remained. Could Peter have contributed in some way, to the death of his father?

Sighing, he did what he always did when he needed to distract and soothe himself.

Not praying, though he frequently chided himself about that.

And not the other thing either, because he'd given it up for Lent.

He picked up his mobile phone and looked to see if anyone had 'liked' his 'Max Kenilworth' profile. They hadn't.

He envied Danny with his new girlfriend, eating pizza no doubt, and watching Game of Thrones.

It made him feel lonely just thinking about it.

All in all, he thought, it hadn't really been the best of days.

Twenty-Six

SUNDAY 14TH APRIL 2019

It was Palm Sunday. And Dido was fascinated by Tyra. She sat, up close and personal, all barrel-like and brindle, snuffling, and staring intently at Elin's aunt as if she might be, rather than have come for, dinner.

Tyra found it unnerving. She was wary of dogs. And she'd mistakenly believed that the low-slung pooch would have no chance of joining her on the sofa. But there was a cushion of the kind you get in church for kneeling. And it seemed to be expressly for the purpose of giving the squat French Bull Terrier a step up. Under the circumstances, it occurred to Tyra that Elin and Dave had been wise to colour match their soft furnishings to the dog.

Dido stared on, wearing an expression that Tyra was struggling to identify.

Was it mistrust? she wondered. Or disdain? The crumpled nose might suggest that. Though it appeared to be a permanent feature. And were pricked ears a good or a bad sign in a dog? She had no idea.

Dave helped her out. 'She likes you!' he said, sounding impressed.

'Really?'

'Yeah. I've never seen her look so adoringly at anybody new before.'

Tyra looked again at the dog. *That* was adoring? Crikey!

'Dinner's almost ready!' called Elin from the galley kitchen. She was nervous that her aunt had finally accepted one of her invitations. She wanted the kitchen to herself to concentrate. And she'd assigned Dave the job of entertaining Tyra. He was impressed by her at close quarters. He thought that she looked 'elegantly wasted', to quote one of his favourite songs from INXS.

He leaned forward from the deep DFS armchair by the fireplace. 'I'm so glad we heard that our neighbours had decided to let their flat with Airbnb. I mean... What perfect timing! I hated to think of you in that hotel room all by yourself all the time. It must have been pretty grim.'

Tyra wasn't sure about the flat idea. Located three doors along the bottom corridor of this creepy old institution, it felt a bit too close for comfort to Elin and Dave. And she hoped they wouldn't want to be dropping in on her all the time. Or, even worse, expect her to return the dinner invitation.

'I quite liked it,' she said. Though in truth, she'd worked her way through the menu at the pub next door. And she was looking forward to being able to shove M&S Ready Meals in the microwave. 'But it will be nice to have a kitchen and a washing machine.'

Dave nodded happily. He took credit for chatting to the

neighbours on his way out with Dido, hearing that they'd be working in Dubai for several months, and managing to snap up a short term let for Tyra.

'I've been really looking forward to meeting you,' he said. 'Elin's been so thrilled to have a proper auntie after all these years you know. I mean... she's got her Auntie Bridget... But she's just an honorary aunt... a friend of Elin's mum.'

'Mm,' Tyra shifted uncomfortably. Dido edged closer as if worried that her new friend may be about to leave. 'I knew Bridget.'

'Really?'

'Yes.' A faint flush rose to her cheeks. She changed the subject. 'So, you're a teacher then? Is that at one of the local schools?'

Dave knew a swift conversational swerve when he heard one. He made a mental note to find out more about the link with Bridget. 'I'm at the Academy just down the road. It's handy. I can cycle or walk there. Help save the planet. I teach Physics and Maths. Elin's mum was Deputy Head there for about five years before she retired. I used to get a lot of ribbing about that.'

Tyra smiled. She liked this good-natured young man and found herself feeling pleased that her niece had found him.

'Do you like it?'

'I love it! Honest to God. There's nothing quite like seeing a kid get fired up about science.'

'I can imagine.' She couldn't really. She'd always hated the sciences at school. But she found his enthusiasm endearing and wanted to share it.

'Elin tells me you studied Literature at UCL.'

'Yes. But I dropped out.'

'How come?'

Tyra thought about this. It was all fairly hazy, to be honest.

'I don't know,' she shrugged, taking the easy way out. 'Sex and drugs and rock n roll, I guess.'

-0-0-0-

Dinner smelt much more appetizing than the dried-up hotplate-offerings of the pub next door to the Value Lodge. It tasted good too.

Dido was leaning against her shin under the table. There was something soothing about the weight of her hot little body, and the way her breathing vibrated through the whole of her. Tyra wasn't sure whether the dog may have fallen asleep in that propped up position. She realised that she was starting to feel protective about her latest fan. She felt worried about moving her leg in case she toppled over.

'So, have you managed to catch up with Elin's mum yet?' asked Dave mischievously after he'd poured large glasses of Aldi's best Argentinian Cabernet Sauvignon for them all.

Elin kicked him furiously under the table.

'Holy crap!!!! I mean... cramp!' he muttered. 'Ouch... Sorry!'

He rubbed his leg under the table.

Dido shifted, and then settled back, heavier than ever.

Tyra took a deep breath, remembering her pep-talk from Max. 'No, but I should do. We've got a quiet week coming up. And I thought I might catch up with a few old friends. Would you mind giving her my number Elin? Unless she's already got it, of course. I guess you or your dad may already have given it to her?'

Elin cursed under her breath. 'She decided to go away for a few days,' she said. 'Though I'm sure she'd still love to hear from you. I'll forward her your number.'

'Thank you.'

'Maybe Elin could forward your number to her Auntie Bridget too?' Dave suggested, mischievously.

Elin looked puzzled. She'd missed the Bridget conversation while she was in the kitchen.

'Were you friends with her too?' she asked. 'She's my Godmother, you know.'

Tyra nodded. 'Though I knew her more as a friend of your mum's. And I doubt that she'd be bothered about seeing me.'

'She was widowed a few years ago,' said Dave, watching carefully for a response.

But he was disappointed.

'I'm sorry to hear that,' said Tyra, taking a lengthy, fortifying gulp of the wine.

-0-0-0-

It felt strange, seeing Elin and Dave standing in their doorway waving as she slid the key into the lock of her new temporary abode.

'Thank you again,' she said, longing to escape inside, but feeling it would be rude to just go in and slam the door.

'Thank you for coming,' called Elin. 'You must come again soon. Dido's besotted with you.'

'I'm fairly taken with her too.'

'Maybe we could take her out for a walk together during the week.'

'Yes, maybe.'

'Bye then.'

'Bye.'

Tyra stepped inside and gently, but firmly closed the door.

Twenty-Seven

It had been a last minute decision for Helen to escape for a few days. Jim, one of her old teaching friends, was a boating fanatic and had a static caravan on the Crouch estuary. She'd phoned him on impulse, doubting that the van would be free on the last weekend before Easter. But she'd been lucky. Jim was getting old and crotchety, and after forty years in the strait-jacket of school holidays, he preferred to use the van at quieter times of year.

So now, just as Tyra finally had the freedom of a late Sunday afternoon to herself, Helen was unpacking her case, and feeling, for the first time in weeks, as if she had space to breathe.

The 'static' was not much smaller than her flat. It had plush, fawn coloured carpet throughout, pristine cream kitchen units, a bathroom, and a TV larger than the one she had at home. As she would have expected in anything owned by Jim, it was so spotlessly clean it made her nervous. There was decking outside with a wooden slatted picnic table and chairs. And the view of the estuary, the distant shoreline of

Wallasea Island, and to the left, the open sea, was already having a lifting effect on her spirits.

It wasn't even all that busy. She could hear a few kids playing ball games outside, but that just felt soothing and reminded her of when her own children were small. She'd been happy then, though she knew that Peter had felt trapped by the demands of his growing family. Sometimes, in Sweden, she would take the kids away to the coast or lakes, to give him the space to work on the compositions he tried to squeeze into the ever narrower crevices of his work and family life. She knew he was frustrated. And she'd felt partly responsible for that. He'd only ever had kids because his father expected it of him. And Elin, so much later than Lucy and Fred, had been an 'accident'. She'd been a happy accident though. Helen loved all three of her children dearly. Even Lucy, who did her best to be unlovable. But she found Elin the easiest to be with. She knew that Peter did too, in his self-absorbed, hopeless kind of way.

And now, she had space extending in front of her like the plain grey expanse of the estuary. She'd come here often on day trips and she planned to spend her time re-treading old ground. There was the quaint harbour town, with its quirky white and pastel shops, red brick clock tower and art deco cinema. And the marina, with its bell-like clanging of boat masts. And the path along the sea wall out of town, where she could see dog walkers out now with scampering puppies or grizzled old plodders, enjoying the feeling of the spring wind in their hair.

She'd felt glad of an excuse not to have to face Bridget in the Five Acres this week too. She knew her friend was impatient with her. She didn't understand how Helen could still be on such friendly terms with Peter, while she was incapable of even saying 'Hello' to Tyra.

Helen felt impatient with herself about it too.

But Peter had never broken her heart. And deep down, she knew that she'd never broken his either, regardless of how many times he might claim that she had. Whereas Tyra... Tyra had been the love of her life.

She looked at her watch. It was 4pm. That sleepy time of day. She could maybe have a snooze on Jim's big comfy double bed. Then wander along the quayside, past the yacht club that looked like an ocean-going liner and find a pub where she wouldn't feel too conspicuous as a lone woman eating a bar meal. She'd brought her own sheets and towels as her old friend had requested. And she'd already changed them, stacking his in a neat pile on one of the empty shelves of the wardrobe, ready to change back before she left.

It seemed impossibly decadent not to have anything to do. But so lovely!

She lay back on the quilt, looking up at the pristine white ceiling. She felt a soft feeling of drowsiness washing over her.

But then her phone vibrated, and a text appeared on the notifications screen. It was from Elin, with Tyra's number.

And suddenly she couldn't sleep. The past was too present for her. The unfinished business too pressing.

-0-0-0-

On the morning after Kristina's funeral, she'd tried to catch Tyra alone, but she knew that she was avoiding her.

Finally, after lunch, when Isak had gone to his study, and Peter had gone to lie down again, she had cornered her in the kitchen.

'We need to talk,' she'd said.

Tyra was scrubbing at an already clean plate, like Lady Macbeth trying to wash away her guilt.

Helen reached out and took it from her hands, placing it on the drainer.

'Now!' she said.

She led Tyra down through the damp grass of the sloping lawn to the summerhouse by the orchard.

Hearing the sharp intake of Tyra's breath, she'd wondered immediately if it had been a mistake. This space had always been Kristina's. Her gardening coat still hung on a hook behind the door. A soft, dusky pink wool blanket was draped over the arm of the sofa. There was a pile of Swedish children's books on the low table in front of it. They must have been left there when Tyra's cousin came to visit with her kids at the start of the summer holiday. A pair of reading glasses lay beside them. The place smelt of cedar and Kristina's signature Chanel 5. And the large windows to the front looked out over the orchard, where the apples seemed to be waiting for her return.

'I'm so sorry!' said Helen. 'This was thoughtless of me. I should never have brought you here.'

But Tyra sank onto the sofa and wrapped herself in the blanket that smelt so perfectly of her mother. And Helen, sensing suddenly that it was ok, wrapped her arms around her too, burying her face in her hair, as Tyra nestled into her like a child needing comfort.

'I don't know how to be without her,' Tyra whispered.

'I know sweetheart.'

'I think we should pick the apples before we go back to London. She would have liked us to do that.'

'Then we'll do it.'

'She used to store them, in the coach house, in straw.'

'We can do that too.'

'I love you. You do know that, don't you?'

'Yes, I love you too.'

'What the hell are we going to do?'

'I don't know.'

Tyra sighed and moved. She opened a cupboard under the side window and placed a half empty bottle of vodka and two shot glasses on the coffee table in front of them. Then she filled both glasses to the rim.

'To Mum!' she said, raising hers steadily towards the lonely coat behind the door. 'She loved it here. It was her favourite bolthole when Dad was in a mood.'

'To Kristina,' said Helen, taking her own glass and sipping at it warily. The pure spirit was too strong for her and made her want to cough.

Tyra knocked back the vodka in her own glass and re-filled it.

She reached affectionately for the top book of the pile on the coffee table. It had a picture of a small boy in a red pompom hat and skis. He was gazing up at a white clad Santa Claus-like figure in a snowy forest. 'Ollie's Ski Trip', she said, translating. 'These were Mum's books when she was a little girl, and she used to read them to me and Peter. We loved them. This one was my favourite, though Peter especially liked the ones with his own name in the title. It's amazing how times have changed. Little Ollie in the book is six when he gets his skis, and his mum makes him sandwiches, and waves him off to spend all day in the forest on his own, talking to strange people.'

She flicked through the pages to where a tri-folded foolscap sheet marked, maybe the last words her mother had ever read.

'Ah,' she said. 'The bit where Ollie realises that Mrs Thaw isn't such a baddie after all.' She smiled through unshed tears. And she was about to return the page marker to its final resting place when some writing on it caught her eye.

It was in Swedish, in blue ink, and signed 'Arne x'.

She opened the sheet. And Helen could see that it was a tour itinerary.

She watched anxiously as Tyra's eyes flicked over place names and dates.

'What is it?' she asked, knowing full well.

Tyra looked back at the short note scrawled on the reverse of the sheet.

She sounded puzzled. 'It's from Arne Karlsson. He was at the funeral yesterday. He used to play saxophone at the Nalen Jazz Club. Mum was with him when she met Dad. Nothing serious. Well, not on her part, at least. Dad sometimes 'joked' that Peter looked suspiciously like him. But that was just rubbish. Mum never had eyes for anyone but Dad from the moment she met him. And Peter looks like *her*. But this is odd. It looks like Arne was hoping Mum might join them on tour this autumn. Obviously he had no idea how totally psycho Dad would have gone about that.'

Helen felt a judder of anxiety running through her. She knew she had to confess. But the thought of it made her feel sick. She took a fortifying sip of vodka. But it just made her feel worse.

'She was thinking of doing the tour,' she said. 'She mentioned it to me.'

Tyra stared at her, horrified. 'When?' she asked.

'The last time I saw her. A few days before the accident.'

She watched the emotions as they swept through Tyra. A cyclone of incomprehension followed by shock and fury.

'Does Peter know?'

'I don't think so. I didn't tell him.'

'And you didn't think to tell me?'

'She swore me to secrecy.'

Seeing Tyra's face darkening with rage, Helen thought, in that moment, that she looked just like her father.

She backed into the corner of the sofa, afraid that she might hit her.

But she 'only' lashed out with words. 'You stupid bloody idiot!' she said, leaping to her feet. 'You came into this family, all sweet and innocent. And you conned us all into loving you. And now you've destroyed us. You know what Dad's like. And Mum trusted you. You should have warned her.'

Helen found her eyes filling with tears.

Tyra turned on her. 'Oh, don't put on the fucking waterworks.'

'I thought she knew what she was doing,' Helen

stammered, trying to defend something she couldn't even defend to herself.

'Mum never knew what she was doing as far as Dad was concerned. You know that! He's a total head-fuck! And, come to think of it, so are you!'

Helen stood, shakily, and reached for Tyra's arm. 'Please, sweetheart. Please don't be like this.'

Tyra shook her away. 'Get off me!' she said, through gritted teeth. 'I wish none of us had ever met you!'

And with that, she stormed out of the summerhouse.

Twenty-Eight

In the present day, Tyra leant back against the door, feeling its cool, painted surface hard against the back of her head. She closed her eyes and drew a long breath, letting it out with a sigh of relief at being alone again at last.

People were problematic for her. She liked some of them. Elin and Danny especially. Even Max, for all his faults. Dave was entertaining and clearly good for Elin, but she sensed that his mischievous nature could make him tricky to be around. And she wasn't at all sure she'd done the right thing in moving practically next door to them.

Wearily, she looked around the hallway. Geometric wallpaper assaulted her eyes, and she averted her gaze rapidly away to the floor, with its black marble tiles that she knew would show every scrap of dust or mud.

The sitting room, straight ahead, was painted the colour of kidney beans, with a black leather sofa and massive wall mounted TV. And 'her' bedroom was in blood orange.

She longed for the cool anonymity of her hotel room.

But she'd made the choice to move and now she needed to make the most of it.

She wandered into the bedroom, where she unlaced and pulled off the boots she'd only just put back on as she left Elin and Dave's. Then she threw herself down on the bed, thinking that, thank goodness, it had ordinary white cotton sheets. Its deep brown satin counterpane reminded her of the melted chocolate Max had wanted her to woo Helen with. She suspected the regular occupants of the flat may have bought the plainer sheets specially for their Airbnb lets, and she was grateful for it. She was grateful for the boarding house white towels in the lime green bathroom too.

The thought of Helen possibly phoning filled her with anxiety. Now she'd opened the door for such a call, it seemed like an impossible thing to deal with. She hoped, simply, that Helen would choose not to phone. That would be the easiest way out for all of them. And it would draw a line under things. Show that she was, as she suspected, unforgivable.

But, if she phoned... And of course, she probably wouldn't. But if she did... What on earth was Tyra going to say?

After more than forty years of silence, 'I'm sorry,' didn't feel like it would hack it. And yet, in some ways, that was all that remained.

She closed her eyes and cast her mind back to her mother's death and the days and nights that followed. And she was sorry more than she could ever say.

Her stupidity haunted her. She'd tried telling herself that she'd been young and grief stricken and bewildered. But none of that came anywhere near excusing her.

She knew she'd felt guilty from the moment she heard the news about her mum. But she'd tried to push it away. She'd imagined that Kristina would always be there, always warm and loving and thrilled to see her when she found the time to visit or arrange a meet-up. She'd known that Helen made more of an effort than she did. She'd even vaguely resented it, feeling excluded from the growing friendship between the two women. But she knew she was excluding herself really. She'd already taken to avoiding Renton Hall, with Isak and his night-time creeping. And she'd started avoiding her mother too after UCL gave her the boot. She'd been a coward and she knew it.

And then there was the guilt about Helen. Her treacherous feelings growing all those years. The attempts to love other women. How futile they all had been. How Helen had filled her dreams. And the knowledge of what would have happened if Peter hadn't tapped on the door that night. She felt flooded with guilt about all that. Because she loved Peter and yet she'd still been willing to betray him.

Now, thinking about her outburst in the summerhouse, Tyra knew that she'd hurled all her guilt at Helen because she couldn't bear it anymore.

She'd been deliberately cruel. Wanted Helen to suffer. Wanted to punish her for the crime of being there for her mother when she wasn't. For simply being herself and 'making' them all love her. From the greater perspective afforded by time and distance and age, she could see how outrageously unfair she'd been that day. And how she'd attacked someone who was already suffering. Though she'd deluded herself that everything she'd said was justified at the time.

She remembered running up the lawn and bursting into Isak's study. He was dictating the latest chapter of his macho rubbish into a Dictaphone for his secretary to type when she came into the office on Monday.

He looked shocked by her sudden appearance. But still he had the presence of mind to switch off the tape. As if he sensed that something was coming that might incriminate him.

She stared breathlessly around the room as he pretended she wasn't there. Isak's study had always been out of bounds to the 'children'. And this was the first time she'd seen it. The wastepaper basket under the desk was full of tissues, and the red Turkish rug on the floor was worn. She noticed that all the books on the shelves above his desk were his own. And it occurred to her that the gilt-framed seascapes on his walls were a strange choice for a man traumatised by seeing his injured brother drown after a torpedo attack on their ship.

Finally, she got her breath back.

'Mum was thinking of going on tour,' she said, accusing him. 'Wasn't she?'

Isak took off his spectacles and rubbed at the sore indentations on either side of his nose.

'I don't know what you mean,' he answered slowly and coldly. He always spoke slowly when he was lying. And he looked angry. She'd never challenged him before. And she'd been neglecting him recently. He didn't like it.

'I mean, she was considering going on tour with Arne Karlsson's band.... Paris... Marseilles... Bruges... Amsterdam... Just for starters.... A three month European tour...'

She waved the foolscap sheet in front of him.

He scoffed. 'Karlsson wanted her to go. He always was sweet on her. But she'd decided not to. She knew she was past it. Knew she'd make a fool of herself.'

Tyra remembered her rage at this final insult to her mother. She felt the blood pounding in her ears. She felt incapable of containing the fury and anguish and dread within her. She needed to stand and fight. Just for once. Now everything was lost. Now it was too late.

'She was a beautiful singer Dad! Beautiful! And you damn well know that… Or maybe you don't… Because come to think of it, you've always been such a tone deaf bastard I can't remember her ever bothering to sing in front of you.'

His chair caught against the edge of the rug and fell as he lunged towards her.

The blow, when it came, was a slap rather than a punch. But it bowled her off her feet and sent her crashing against the ancient wood-panelled wall of the study.

Isak's face was purple, bull-like, blood pulsing in his temples. His fists were clenched.

'How dare you speak like that to your father?' he demanded.

All the times she'd seen him like this flashed back to her. With her mother. With Peter. But never before with her. His cursed favourite.

'If you want respect then maybe you should stop jerking off over me when you're 'sleep walking' then,' she spat back, reaching for the handle of the door. 'And over Helen too. And every other young woman who has the misfortune to stay over for the night.'

Isak caught her by the neck of her T-shirt. 'You filthy little pervert!' he yelled in her face. 'How dare you? After what I saw at your window from the garden when I couldn't sleep last night? With your brother's girlfriend. You pair of filthy sluts!'

Tyra felt her knees go weak. She lashed backwards at Isak with her elbow and shoved him away, yanking the door open and escaping out into the hallway.

Her father's final words rang in her ears as she raced down the corridor to the stairs.

'Thank God your mother didn't live to see what you've become. Evil little bitch. Get out of my house. Now. Before I kill you.'

-0-0-0-

Somehow, she'd found herself in a gay bar. She'd got back to London on the train. Pacing at the station. Running up elevators on the underground. Staring down commuters who'd caught her eye, concerned. She had her overnight bag with her. She'd tossed her clothes into it and left everything else. She didn't think she cared about any of it anymore.

And now it was Saturday evening. The bar was filling up. The people with shopping bags at the end of a hard afternoon in Oxford Street were already drifting home when Tyra arrived, and the night owls were starting to arrive. The air was heavy with smoke and the greasy Seventies smells of Scampi and Chips and Chicken in the Basket.

A young woman was sitting by the jukebox, where 'Rock the Boat' by The Hues Corporation was somebody's favourite. She kept looking across at Tyra as if she were trying to catch her eye. She looked a bit like Helen, though not so pretty. And she looked lonely and a bit lost. Eventually, when a jovial group of young queens asked her whether the seats at the table were taken, or could they sit down, she came over and joined Tyra at the bar. 'Can't hear myself think with that lot!' she said good-naturedly. She was wearing flared denim jeans with an embroidered cheesecloth top. It was unbuttoned, by accident or design, to show just a glimpse of flesh-toned bra underneath. She smelt of Aqua Manda and beer.

At the table she'd just vacated, the boys screeched with laughter.

Tyra could see what she meant.

'Are you the singer with Alstrom?'

'I suppose I am.' She was very drunk by then and not feeling very courteous.

But her admirer was drunk too, and beyond the stage of finding coolness discouraging.

'Can I buy you a drink?' she asked.

Tyra shrugged. 'If you like.'

'I saw you on stage at the 'Big Picnic' in Richmond Park last year. I was with my ex. I thought you were great.'

Tyra remembered it. Outside gigs were always risky in England. But it had been hot that day. And her mother had still been alive.

'Thanks.'

'My name's Cindy by the way.'

'Like the dress-up doll?'

'No, with a 'C'. Short for Lucinda.'

'Okay.'

'And your name is…?'

'Tyra.'

'You don't say much do you?'

'I'm just drunk, that's all.'

Cindy gestured to the barman, pointing to Tyra's glass,

mouthing 'Same again,' and ordering a lager for herself. Tyra felt bad because she was drinking Southern Comfort and it was expensive. But the guilt soon wore off. She felt indifferent to her effect on Cindy and wished she didn't. The poor woman was obviously upset about the ex. And now she was having the misfortune to hit on someone who couldn't give a damn.

She emptied the glass in one and put it down on the drip mat on the bar. She'd been staring at that mat for a long time now. It was green and soggy, with Carlsberg written in white. She wondered if it would be imprinted on her memory forever. And it was.

'So?' asked Cindy. 'What's pissed you off? Hopefully the band haven't dumped you?'

'Nope.'

'Girlfriend trouble?'

'Something like that.'

Cindy looked indecently pleased at this.

'She probably wasn't worth it then…. Like mine… Look, do you fancy to come back to my place? My housemates are out for the night. And I've got a half bottle of that stuff back at the house….' She nodded towards Tyra's empty glass as if unsure that she'd be a big enough draw without it.

She may have been right.

'Where's your place?'

'Smith Street. It's about 5 minutes away.'

Cindy raised an eyebrow in a clumsy attempt at looking seductive.

Tyra slid off her barstool, picked up her bag, and allowed herself to be led away.

-0-0-0-

Cindy was kissing her as soon as they got into the house. She was a passionate and slightly sloppy kisser, leaving a trail of saliva that Tyra could feel drying on her face and neck. It reminded her of when she was young, and her aunts on her father's side would spit on a hanky to wipe chocolate or ice cream from her face. She tried not to think of that. And she tried not to compare these kisses with Helen's so much sweeter ones the night before.

She felt Cindy's hand grasping hers and pulling her through a hallway floored with grubby Lino and bristling with bikes and hooks and outdoor coats like the old cloakroom at school. She smelt damp wool and joss sticks, and... somewhere, she thought, there must be a cat. Though that was probably out on the prowl, like the other residents of the house.

She wondered who'd lived here before. Who'd put the faded 1930's wallpaper on the staircase. Who'd endured the war and the blitz in this house.

Cindy pulled her into her bedroom. A variation on almost every house-share bedroom Tyra had ever seen. Wallpaper painted over with magnolia. Pink Floyd, Janis Joplin, and vintage Votes for Women posters on the walls.

Cindy drew the thin brown curtains.

Tyra dropped her bag on the floor, and pulled Cindy down onto the bed, grasping her at the waist, as much to keep out of the way of the kissing as anything. Encouraged by this apparent interest, Cindy yanked the cheesecloth blouse over her head. Then she whipped down her bra straps, offering her left breast to be fondled, while unzipping Tyra's jeans and thrusting her hand inside.

Tyra turned her head just in time as the mouth came down towards her again and she felt instead the surprisingly erotic wetness of a tongue in her ear, just as Cindy entered her.

In her confused state, and coming far sooner than was courteous, she wasn't sure which part of her Cindy was referring to when she whispered, 'God, you're wet for me!' against her earlobe.

-0-0-0-

Later, waking from a short, exhausted sleep, Tyra extricated herself from her snoring partner's arms and went in search of the bathroom. She'd been glad that they'd had the house to themselves through the ear shattering noisiness of Cindy's exhortations for 'Harder'… 'Faster'… 'There…. Yes… there… just there…' And she'd braced herself for things to get even noisier. But just when she'd thought she couldn't keep going any longer without another stiff drink, there had come the rather anti-climactic, low-key, wordless something that was a cross between a squeak and a groan that gave her permission to stop. Thank God!

She'd figured that if the cat hadn't been out when they arrived, but simply snoozing in a cosy corner somewhere, it must surely have fled in terror by now. And she was slightly surprised that the neighbours hadn't called the police.

The bathroom was as she had expected it to be. High Victorian ceiling. Ancient tiles. Toilet with string where a chain once was. And cold. How did it manage to be so cold when it was only September?

Thinking of that made her long for the house she shared with Peter and Max and Danny, where, at least, there was central heating. She tiptoed back to Cindy's room with excuses at the ready. But she didn't need them. Her once-off lover was still fast asleep and now sprawled on her side, across the whole of the single bed, hugging her pillow.

Tyra weighed up her options. Should she do a runner now? Or do the 'decent' thing and wait till the morning? She compromised, finding a notepad and pen on Cindy's desk, and writing 'Sorry, had to get home. Ring me, okay?' Then, after hovering for some time over the page, she added her phone number and signed, 'Ty x.'

She didn't want Cindy to ring. But even drunk, she couldn't bring herself to just disappear, like a thief in the night.

She carried her bag under her arm down the stairs to avoid scuffing the wallpaper.

And as she let herself out into the weed-choked front garden and through the gate onto the street, she heard her father's voice again, ringing in her head.

'Thank God your mother didn't live to see what you've become.'

-0-0-0-

That Sunday, with Peter still not back from Renton Hall, she built a bonfire in the garden with her father's books, his letters to her, and all the photographs she had of him. She was careful, when the photos also had images of Peter, or her mother, or sundry other friends or family members, to cut her father out without damaging the others. Danny and Max exchanged shrugs and went back to smoking weed and watching Tom and Jerry cartoons on TV.

By teatime, when Peter arrived home, she was drunk again, if she had ever been fully sober from the day before.

She thought, as he peeped cautiously round the door of her bedroom, that he was, and always had been, so much prettier than she was. She thought it even more now that her mother was gone, and only Peter, who looked so much like her, remained.

'Ty….. What the hell happened between you and Dad?' he asked, concerned.

The room looked like it had been burgled. Books and papers were everywhere, family photos gone.

Tyra was lying on the bed. She stared at the ceiling, too ashamed to look at her brother.

'I don't want to talk about it,' she said.

'Was it about your sexuality? Did you come out to him?'

'Kind of.'

'Not great timing Sis!'

'No!' she gritted her teeth, wanting him to go and leave her alone to chew over her misery.

'He'll come round. You know how he is.'

'I don't want to talk about it Pete.'

'Ok!' he raised his hands in surrender. 'Do you fancy something to eat. Helen's staying for tea. We're just going to do something quick like beans on toast or something.'

She realised that she was hungry. Hadn't eaten all day. But couldn't face Helen.

'I'll get something later,' she said.

'Okay.' He backed out of the room, presumably to report to Helen that she was 'upset' and wasn't coming down. On the way out, he remembered, 'Helen asked me to tell you… We picked the apples, and put them in straw, in the coach house, like you wanted.'

-0-0-0-

She never really pulled herself back after that weekend.

Strangely, it was a creative time. Songs tumbled from her. And on stage and off she had an intensity that seemed to make her irresistible to women.

Alstrom started to attract the attention of A&R men. As the months drifted by there were a couple of appearances on TV. Bigger gigs. And finally, Peter's dream come true. The recording contract with a small sympathetic record company, long since gobbled up by a more successful beast, with the savvy to sell rights for 'You Watching Me,' to the producers of 'Fördömelse'.

It could have been a good time for Tyra. A time to honour her mum's memory. Express her creativity. Maybe even find a way of making things right with Helen.

But she didn't. Instead, she moved out of the house to reduce the torment of seeing her brother with his girlfriend. She drank too much. And took too many drugs. Sometimes, she wondered if there was anything she'd never tried.

Cindy phoned, but didn't last long. The last Tyra heard of her; she'd hooked up with another of her one-night stands.

She felt glad for them and hoped it would last. But she didn't tell them that.

She became erratic and careless and arrogant.

When she was sober, she still hated being in the spotlight. But she hated herself more.

She was an accident waiting to happen.

And when it came, she wrecked things for everyone.

-0-0-0-

Tyra still had no idea how to atone for all that.

Not with Peter. And especially not with Helen.

She kept looking at her phone, but no call came.

Time hung heavy on her hands.

She switched on her keyboard and waited for a song.

Twenty-Nine

Helen lay in bed, staring at the clean white ceiling of the caravan. Distantly, she heard cars returning to their parking spaces beside holiday homes, children chattering, adult voices lower, murmuring. And as the night progressed, a silence deeper than she ever heard at home, where the faint sounds of the other flat dwellers were always there to remind her that she was not alone.

She remembered the time after Kristina's funeral as a continuation of the horror she'd lived with since she heard the news of her death.

After Tyra stormed from the summerhouse, she'd stayed there for a long time, not daring to return to the Hall, wanting to feel some comfort in a place that Kristina had always loved. But she couldn't feel any comfort there at all.

She'd drunk a lot of the vodka, not thinking that anyone would notice its absence now. And Peter hadn't seen that she was unsteady on her feet when she finally plucked up the courage to zigzag up the lawn and seek him out.

He'd been woken from his sedated sleep by the raised voices in the study. But she'd found him still huddled in his room, too frightened to emerge, used to hiding away when he heard the booming fury of his father.

He didn't know that Tyra had gone. And he was distraught when he discovered it. It wasn't how things were supposed to be. Tyra had always been the one who tried to make everything alright for him.

But not anymore. Helen lost count of the times she tried to speak to her. She considered writing, but she was scared to commit anything to paper. She didn't trust Tyra not to show it to Peter in her rage. She barely recognised the young woman she had grown to love.

On stage, when she was coherent, Tyra was on fire. The purity of her voice belied the stark despair of her songs. It was as if she held up a mirror to the audience, expressing what they'd never dared to say. They loved her for it. And on bad nights, not so many at first, but more and more as the months wore on, they forgave her.

She began to fight with Peter. Always the perfectionist, he hated it when she spoiled the show.

Max and Danny didn't care. They could bash out a beat indefinitely. Sometimes, even on a bad night, Tyra would catch up with them and snatch victory from the jaws of defeat. They were happy so long as the money and the gigs and the drugs and the girls kept coming. Brian kept his head down, and felt the pain of Peter, who he'd always, secretly loved. 'Like a son', of course.

Helen had watched all this from the side lines. She arrived late to the dressing room on the night Tyra punched Peter for 'lecturing her'. She held a damp towel to the bridge of his nose, wondering if he needed an X-Ray as he bled copiously into the sink.

Tyra had already moved to a shared house in Leyton. She said she needed 'space'. But she never seemed to be alone.

Then the fledgling record label signed them.

They recorded their album.

In the studio, away from the crowds, Tyra managed to hold things together. Her timekeeping was erratic. But her singing was good. Maybe better than it had ever been.

Helen, hearing the reports each day from Peter, began to hope that she was settling down.

But then came the tour…

They were scheduled to start with ten cities in the UK, followed by a two month foray into Northern and Western Europe.

They'd played some of those places before.

But this was different. The venues were bigger. They had the publicity budget of a record company behind them. And they were promoting an album. Finally, it felt like they were on the verge of something big.

Even Danny and Max were excited.

Brian's mum was worried that he'd become famous and move out.

And Helen was hoping the break from Peter would give her some welcome time alone to think about their relationship.

-0-0-0-

The tour was scheduled to kick off in London, with a gig at the Marquee.

She arrived home from school to find the telephone ringing. It was Peter, shouting that Tyra hadn't turned up for the sound check. He was furious and frightened. He'd phoned the house in Leyton and got some 'stroppy bisom' who'd told him to stop shouting, and then put the phone down on him when he wouldn't. Helen could imagine that his panicky aggression wouldn't have played well with his sister's new housemates. She'd tried to reassure him. Reminded him that Tyra always got there in the end. Told him she'd go and hurry her along.

It was rush hour. And she struggled to find a parking space in the street full of multi-occupancy houses. But finally, she was striding up the weed-choked path to Tyra's place.

She remembered taking a deep breath to fortify herself before ringing the bell. She'd felt anxious seeing Tyra ever since the row in the summerhouse.

A thick set woman with short henna-red hair answered. Helen didn't recognise her. She was wearing a denim shirt, and jeans. She looked grumpy.

Helen suspected that this was the 'stroppy bisom' Peter had annoyed earlier.

'Is Tyra in?'

The woman shrugged and wandered back through the hallway and into what must be the shared sitting room of the house. 'She's probably upstairs,' she said as she went back to the Vesta curry she'd been eating in front of the TV.

'Which room?'

'Sorry... Thought I'd seen you here before. It's the one furthest from the top of the stairs.'

'Thanks.'

She ran upstairs and tapped gently on the closed door.

'Tyra!' she called. 'Tyra, are you in there?'

There was no answer.

She turned the handle and peered round the door. It took a while for her eyes to adjust to the semi-darkness of the room.

It stank of sweat and alcohol. The curtains were drawn and illuminated pale blue by the fading day outside. The only light within came from the display of the hi-fi and the numbers of the LED alarm clock.

Tyra was on the unmade bed, not in it. She appeared to be asleep.

Helen didn't want to jolt her awake by switching on the bedside lamp.

She knelt on the floor, soft beneath her knees with scattered clothes.

'Hey… Sleepy head.' She felt swamped by the tenderness she'd always felt for this troubled young woman. She could barely see through the gloom. But she didn't like her stillness, or the shallowness of her breathing. She touched her hand and felt the skin cool beneath hers. She shook her arm, feeling panic rising. 'Come on Baby. Don't frighten me!'

Still, Tyra didn't move.

'Tyra! Come on now. Stop dicking around with me!'

She shook her harder and felt tears of panic starting in her eyes.

Then she stood and switched on the lamp and saw the relics of Tyra's increasingly desperate attempts to calm her crippling pre-concert nerves. The whiskey bottle, the prescription diazepam, and the scorched tin foil, with lighter and straw.

She stared at her on the bed, still breathing…. just.

She almost fell down the stairs in her rush.

'Where's your phone?' she yelled at the startled woman who had let her in. 'I need to call an ambulance.'

-0-0-0-

She'd wanted to stay, but Peter sent her home. 'She's done enough damage,' he said. 'You have to work tomorrow. And I'm not going to be going anywhere… Let's face it.'

He was cold with rage and grief and she hadn't dared argue with him.

'If she recovers from this I'll fucking kill her myself,' he muttered as Helen squeezed his shoulder and left.

It was the last time she'd seen Tyra. On life support. In the Intensive Care Unit of Whipps Cross Hospital.

In the waiting room, where she stopped to give the update that nothing had changed, Danny and Max had given her hugs. Brian had patted her hand. Somehow their love for Tyra was winning over what she had done to them.

'Are you going to be okay?' asked Max. 'At home, on your own, I mean.' For once she felt sure he was not propositioning her.

She'd nodded. 'Thanks, but I'll be fine,' she said. 'Bridget will be there.'

But Bridget knew nothing of the events of the evening. And by the time Helen got home, she was already fast asleep in bed. So Helen had sobbed the shock she couldn't show into her pillow, watching the clock tick away the endless hours until the morning, when, at 6.07 am, Peter rang to tell her that his sister had regained consciousness, and he hadn't killed her yet.

Three weeks later, Tyra left the country.

She never even came to say goodbye.

Thirty

MONDAY 15TH APRIL 2019

Now Peter had almost finished getting everything in order. He'd signed the papers from the solicitor. The house was on the market. Clearance people would come and take away the furniture after he'd gone.

Helen had already taken everything she wanted. He was sure of that.

And so, there were just final visits to be made.

He felt better, now he'd made the decision. He was tired of feeling like a burden to everyone.

Calmly, he took his Spaghetti Bolognese out of the microwave and carried it through to the living room on a tray. He was fed up with sitting in the conservatory and gazing through the steamed up windows at the garden. And anyway, he liked to watch Sky News while he ate. He'd read somewhere that it was better to avoid the news if you're depressed. But he'd never taken any notice of that.

His first thought, when he saw Notre Dame burning that night, was to phone Helen. They'd honeymooned in Paris, queued to visit the cathedral, cruised by candlelight on the Seine beneath it. It felt like something they'd loved together. And now it was on fire, and maybe would be lost forever.

Tears stung his eyes as he watched the smoke and flames rising, and the footage, over and over of the spire collapsing.

He set his tray aside, the food untouched.

Helen had become his only safe harbour in those years since his mother and Tyra had gone.

He reached for his phone and rang her.

-0-0-0-

She let the call go to voicemail.

She hadn't turned on her TV, or she would have answered. She'd had a quiet day. Late up and drinking coffee while gazing out of the window at the sun sparkling on the waters of the estuary. Watching the white sails of yachts, and flocks of seagulls rising in clouds. She'd made sandwiches and walked out along the natural embankment of the sea wall, past rotting hulls of boats and orange fishing nets tangled with seaweed and plastic bottles on the thin strips of beach. The day had been sunny. Not particularly warm, but perfect for walking. And it had been good to let herself just be there in the present, away from everyone and everything that felt so impossibly complicated back home.

Now she was wondering whether to venture into the town, or just warm up a can of soup, and cosy down for the night with the natural light show of the sunset over the estuary, and a few chapters of the latest Hilary Mantel before an early night to bed.

In the end, she chose the latter. She felt nicely tired after her walk, and the caravan was snug with the fire on.

Peter didn't leave a message, so she assumed it wasn't urgent.

She didn't see the fire at Notre Dame until the morning after. And by then, the cathedral had been saved.

Thirty-One

THURSDAY 18TH APRIL 2019

Peter felt his anxiety ramping as he stood at Tyra's door. He'd already had his lunch with Elin. Dave, thankfully, had sensed a serious conversation coming on, and made himself scarce.

And now he'd been packed off down the corridor with a whispered 'Good luck Dad!' that hadn't exactly filled him with confidence.

'How hard can this be?' he asked himself, squaring up to the door, and jiggling from one foot to the other like a boxer preparing for the biggest fight of his life.

He took a deep breath and rang the bell.

It was strange to see his sister with greying hair. And it was shorter than he remembered her ever wearing it in the 'old days'. Her eyes seemed paler somehow. She was growing old, like him. But her dress sense hadn't changed. Faded jeans, a sweatshirt, grey socks. And she looked healthier than he remembered. Elin had assured him that she'd seen no sign of illicit substances. And he tended to trust Elin's judgment.

Tyra looked startled to see him, but she collected herself quickly.

'Hey, Pete!' she said, standing back to let him in. 'I've been meaning to come round.'

He scoffed at this. He couldn't help himself.

'Yeah, sure,' he said. 'That would be for…. Now, let me see…. around forty three years, would it?' His voice dripped with the sarcasm she probably deserved. But then the decoration of the flat came to her rescue. 'Christ!' he gasped, as the full horror of the hallway hit him. 'Does this wallpaper come with a trigger warning?'

'You should see the other rooms!'

'Ber-loody hell!' he gasped, peeping round each of the doors as she opened them for him to see.

She laughed, and he could see her easing up a little. She was on safe ground with the wallpaper.

'Do you want a cup of tea? Or coffee? Or I've got something stronger if you're not driving?'

He shook his head. 'I'd better stick to tea, I think.'

'Do you still have two sugars?'

'Are you kidding me? I'm a total 'New Man' now. Weak, black and no sugar at all please. And if you've got Rooibos, even better.'

'No, sorry, I've only got bog standard English Breakfast, I'm afraid. Red Bush always tastes like Germolene to me. But if I'd known you were coming, I could have got you some. And some squashed fly biscuits to go with it.'

He laughed. 'Well, it just so happens…' He presented a packet of Garibaldi's from the black messenger bag slung over his shoulder. 'Mum always said it was bad manners to visit without bringing a gift.'

-0-0-0-

Perched on the enormous sofa, sipping from a designer mug, with the plate of Garibaldi biscuits between them, he felt unable to escape from the shadowy alter-him in the TV screen. It reminded him of a game called 'Mirrors', that he and Tyra used to play when they were kids. And it seemed to reproach him, reminding him that he'd been good looking once, and hadn't held on to that as well as his sister.

Another failure, he thought, grimly. Dad would have been proud.

Tyra, tucked as far away as possible from him at the far corner of the sofa, seemed as ill at ease as he was.

'Have you been to see Elin?' she asked, desperate for conversational openings.

'Yes, I went round for lunch. She's been nagging me for ages. I think she imagines that I don't eat when I'm on my own.'

'And do you?'

'Of course I do. Isn't that what Ready Meals are for?'

Tyra laughed. 'My sentiments entirely,' she said.

They looked at each other fondly, and for a moment, it was as if the years fell away, and they were young again, home from school, with long warm summer days ahead of them.

Tyra was the first to drop the gaze.

'I was sorry to hear about Helen,' she said.

He supposed Elin had told her. Though it could just as easily have been Max.

'Were you?'

She flinched at the anger in his retort.

'What the hell does that mean? Of course I was. I wish you'd told me. I could have…'

She tailed off, shamed by the knowledge that she probably wouldn't have done anything.

And Peter saw it. He made a short, scoffing noise. 'What?' he asked. 'What could you have done? I suppose you could have come home to see me, or picked up the phone, at least. But you'd probably just have done sweet FA like you always do.'

Tyra shut up and drank her tea.

'I don't blame her,' he said suddenly. 'Helen, I mean. There have been so many times when I could hardly bear living with myself, you know.'

'Yes,' said Tyra. 'I know how that feels. But seriously… How have you been? It must have been a tough few months for you. Helen going. And finding Dad like that.'

He shrugged. 'It would have been nice if you'd come to the funeral.'

'I couldn't face it.'

He shook his head. 'You never used to be a coward Ty. And you could have come to support me. And the kids…. And Helen.'

'Yes,' she looked away. 'I'm sorry. I should have come.'

There was a long silence.

'I was sorry to hear that Brian died too,' she said, finally. 'What happened? Max and Danny don't seem to know.'

'No, it was only me that kept in touch with him. He had Parkinson's. He died last year, about a fortnight after Helen left.'

'I'm sorry. I liked him.'

'Yes, he liked you too. He was gutted when you bailed on us.'

There it was again, the bitterness. He found he couldn't stay away from it. Like a dog returning to its own vomit.

'I'm sorry Pete. I don't know what you want from me.'

'An explanation would be good, for a start.'

He took a long swig of his tea and bit into one of the biscuits. He didn't want to be like this. He knew he could have done things differently. He could have seen the writing on the wall. And he could have got another singer. He knew that Tyra hated being in the spotlight. He'd exploited her. Given her drugs to take the fear away. Just as their parents had given her alcohol, so she wouldn't see the shadows in their 'perfect' life.

'I can't explain, truly. I was just a complete mess. I needed to get away.'

'To 'find' yourself?'

'I guess.'

'And did you?'

'Kind of… But, in retrospect, I think there may have been quicker ways.'

Peter spluttered with laughter at that. 'You always were a mistress of understatement,' he said.

She joined in with the laughter, happy enough to be the butt of it.

'I really did mean to come round to see you,' she said.

'Since I've been back in England, I mean. But I kept hoping you'd come back to the band. Especially once we had Elin on board. I know she kept you in the loop. And it's not the same without you.'

Peter looked away. 'I'm not up to it,' he said. 'How are Max and Danny shaping up? They were pretty ragged at our first rehearsals.'

Tyra shrugged. 'They're good,' she said. 'Much better than me. At least they've been playing all these years. Max has his band at church. And Danny plays a lot at the studios. I'm the weakest link. But I think we're getting the old Alstrom magic back.'

For a second, Peter looked disappointed. But he collected himself quickly.

'They're probably happier without me,' he said. 'Danny in particular. He never liked me.'

With Peter, all roads led back to the same old insecurities. People didn't like him. Or, even if they did, they liked Tyra better.

'Don't be daft!' she said.

'I'm not! He thought I was a racist.'

'No, he didn't! Not really. He thought we were both spoilt Trust Fund Brats. And you just got off on a bad foot with him because his girlfriend fancied you.'

This was news to Peter. 'Which girlfriend?'

'Susan, of course.'

'Susan? You're pulling my leg!'

Tyra shook her head. 'Are you seriously telling me you didn't notice her walking around the house in her undies whenever Danny and Helen weren't around?'

'Well, yes, but I just thought that's how she was. And I always made sure I looked away.'

Tyra laughed. 'Well I bloody didn't, I'll tell you! But didn't you find it odd, the way she'd nestle up to you on the sofa and stroke your hair?'

'I just thought she was being affectionate.'

Tyra shook her head in wonderment.

He sighed and took another bite of Garibaldi. Now Tyra had pointed it out to him, he was running through a whole Timothy Lea novel's worth of failed seduction attempts by Danny's tone deaf ex-girlfriend.

'Crikey!' he said. 'No wonder Dan didn't like me!'

Tyra smiled fondly, and he imagined she was thinking how clueless he'd always been as far as women were concerned.

'You were very pretty back then Pete. And you never knew it. All the girls fancied you.'

He knew she was trying to ride the momentum of his good mood.

But something kept dragging him back.

'Apart from when they fancied *you*,' he said. 'Dad told me about you and Helen, by the way.'

He took a deep breath. This was really the conversation he'd come to have with her.

'When Helen left, I put off telling him for ages,' he said. 'I felt like such a loser. And I waited till I was sure she wasn't going to come back. But when it became clear that she'd gone for good, I knew I had to bite the bullet. He took great pleasure in bringing me up to speed. He told me what he'd seen on the night of Mum's funeral. He said Helen only married me because she wanted the Alström money and she couldn't have you. I'm surprised he never said it before. It gave him such joy to rub my nose in it. You know how he was. He always enjoyed hurting me.'

Tyra stared at him. Of course, she should have realised. It was almost surprising that Isak had kept it to himself for so long. Maybe, initially, it had been his insurance policy. Something to hold over her to make sure she kept his guilty secrets. But by last year, he must have known that time was running out, and seized his first opportunity to inflict maximum pain on his son.

'Anyway,' Peter continued. 'It didn't work that time. It actually made it all feel just that little bit better. It must have been such a disappointment for his 'big reveal' to fall so flat. But I know Helen was never a gold digger. And it helped to think that maybe no man would have held her attention for long.'

Tyra's eyes softened with sympathy. She wasn't sure whether a different man may have held Helen. And in many ways it felt irrelevant now. Because Peter was the man she'd chosen. 'The two of you created a beautiful family together,' she said.

'Yes,' he acknowledged. 'We did, didn't we.'

He thought of his children, and how, in many ways, they'd all surpassed him. But he didn't want to let Tyra off the hook with his beautiful family.

'How long?' he asked. 'Tell me the truth now. How long were you seeing each other behind my back? How long were you making a fool of me? And who else knew…? Danny maybe? Or Max? I don't think Brian could have known because I think he'd have warned me. But Bridget… for sure. Helen told her everything. And she'd have enjoyed seeing her joining the 'sisterhood'. She never did think I was good enough for her precious friend.'

Tyra reached out and put her hand on his. He flinched it away, almost knocking the Garibaldis off the plate.

She sighed. 'It wasn't like that,' she said. 'I loved her for years. But she had absolutely no idea. I'm sure it never even crossed her mind to think of me in that way. She was too much in love with you. And I never, ever tried anything, I promise. I think she would have been horrified if I had. Or at least clueless, like you were with Susan.' She paused, hoping he'd see the humour in that. But he didn't. So she went on. 'It was a weird time you know. You were absorbed in the band, and she was living such a different life. She was doing a stressful job. Working long hours. I think she thought you weren't really interested in her anymore. And I think if you're honest with yourself, she was right.'

She hesitated for a moment, wondering if he might acknowledge what she had said. But he didn't. So she continued. She wanted to express what had happened without trying to excuse it.

'I don't think you ever really loved her like I did. I think she was a convenience to you. Someone to pick you up when you were down. A badge of honour to signal to the other guys that you weren't really the sad sap you always suspected they thought you were. You didn't sit with her when she was at her wit's end with a class she couldn't control. Or when one of her students committed suicide. You never understood that she needed to get to bed at a reasonable time.... Except when it suited you. And you pushed her away when Mum died. It hurt her when you automatically turned to me, you know. You never once recognised that she was grieving too, and might need some comfort from you... Or might get comfort from grieving together with you. So, I don't know how it happened, but gradually, we just became closer. And the times were changing too, of course. I was gay, and Bridget was gay. And I guess something that hadn't seemed even possible to her started to feel like a possibility.

Peter was quiet. Staring at the floor. He wanted to hold on to his anger. But he could see that she was right.

'But how long?' he persisted. 'How long did it go on for?'

She felt flooded with despair. She doubted that he'd believe her. And cursed her father's malice. 'Just that one night,' she said. 'Just what Dad saw.'

He looked at her then, surprised. 'That's what *she* said too.

Tyra was shocked. 'You mean... You've already discussed this with Helen?'

'Yes. I asked her about it as soon as Dad spilled the beans. And she said the same. But I didn't believe her.'

'Well, why would you believe me then? We could have cooked up the story between us, after all.'

'I know,' he said. 'But you're right. I never loved or trusted Helen as much as I should have. Nowhere near as much as I've always loved and trusted you.'

Tyra stared at him. 'So why the hell didn't you set her free Peter? Why marry her?'

He shrugged. 'I suppose you could ask her the same question. And it would probably be the same answer. You'd gone. And Mum had gone. And each of us was all the other one had left.'

Thirty-Two

By four o'clock, Dave was still not back from his visit to his mum. And Elin could bear the suspense no longer.

She'd discovered that if she walked Dido on the grass slope behind the asylum building, she could get a good view into Tyra's sitting room. It was a gloomy room with very little direct sunlight and the light was almost always on. It would create a perfectly lit stage set for any drama that might be happening within.

'Hey Dido, walkies!' she announced in the hyper-excited tone that people use to con their pets into thinking that walks round the block are going to be fun.

Dido wasn't easily conned. She looked up sleepily from the sofa. It wasn't walk time, and her two favourite exercise buddies, Dave and Tyra weren't there. She tucked her nose back under her chubby rump and prepared to drift off again.

'Let's go meet Dave!' said Elin.

The dog's head cocked at the beloved name.

'DAVE!' said Elin again, shamelessly.

Dido untangled herself and ambled over to have her lead clipped on.

Elin told herself she should feel guilty, lying to the dog. But she didn't.

-0-0-0-

There was no sign of her dad in Tyra's room though. Her aunt was sitting alone before her keyboard. The French doors were open just a couple of inches, and Elin edged closer.

Believing herself free from the glare of an audience, Tyra was singing. It wasn't a regular Alstrom song. Or, at least, not one that Elin recognised.

She strained to hear the words…

All my life, I've walked alone.

Stumbled through the night, frightened to come home.

Made so many big mistakes.

Lost my heart.

I felt it break.

Taken all there is to take.

And all the time your voice has called me home….

Dido snuffled contentedly around the decking, lulled by the sound of Tyra's voice, and following the interesting scent trails of the little creatures who lived beneath.

Elin hoped no-one would see as she found the Recorder App on her mobile and held it to the gap.

Tyra stopped and restarted the song several times, working on it, changing chords, changing words.

Finally, she seemed content with what she'd created. She sat for a minute or so in silence, deep in thought, or possibly even prayer. But then she turned and saw Dido peering myopically through the glass panel of the door just as the dog caught sight of her.

She leant across and slid the door wider.

And Elin landed in an undignified heap at her aunt's feet.

Tyra helped her up as she stuffed the phone back in her pocket.

'Is Dad still here?' she asked when she was upright again. She pretended to peer around the room as if she hadn't already been doing that from outside.

'No, he didn't stay long,' Tyra was distracted, tickling under Dido's armpits.

'Oh... I thought he was coming back to mine. I've got a couple of casseroles in the freezer for him. And I didn't want him to miss me while I was out with Dido.'

'Oh, yes, he said you were scared he wasn't eating properly.'

Tyra straightened up rather creakily, and brushed dog hair from her jeans.

'He said he was going to call in on Max on the way home,' she said.

'Oh,' Elin brightened. 'Is he coming back to the band?'

'I don't think so. He said he needed to talk to him about something.'

Elin's heart sank at this. She'd decided it was better to try and forget her misgivings about the night of her grandad's death. And she was rather regretting ever discussing it with Max. She hoped he hadn't broken his promise about confidentiality and phoned her dad.

'Oh... okay. Well, it looks like he's missed out on his casseroles... What was the song by the way? I didn't recognise it.'

Tyra's face clouded. 'Could you hear it from outside? I hope I haven't been disturbing the neighbours.'

'No... It was only faint. Is it a new one?'

'Yes,' Tyra looked edgy. 'It's just some ideas I was messing around with.'

'Well... It sounded good. I guess I'd better carry on with Dido's walk. She was desperate to come out.'

Dido glanced up from where she'd curled herself at Tyra's feet. She pretended she hadn't heard.

'They make you out to be such liars,' sighed Elin sheepishly. 'Did everything go okay with Dad, by the way?'

'Sure!' Tyra shrugged. 'It was a good start anyway, I think.... Did you send my number to your mum?'

'Yes, why? Hasn't she got back to you?'

'No.'

'She's maybe not got a good signal where she is. She's due back tomorrow.'

'Okay.'

Tyra nudged Dido gently with her foot.

'I think it's walkies time,' she said to the dog.

Outside, Elin felt the first giant spots of rain.

She glanced up at the sky and then down at the decking where the raindrops were spreading like ink spots on the wood.

'I think we'd better go home for our raincoats first,' she said.

Thirty-Three

The Choir Mistress had a crush on Max. He hadn't noticed. She wasn't his usual 'type', being a fifty-something widow with a couple of grown up kids. A lifelong member of the Church, Sylvia Darrowby had nursed her husband, Gerard, through many years of cancer. She hid her loneliness behind a generic middle-aged ladies haircut, heavy rimmed glasses, and dowdy clothes.

Max had been so kind during Gerard's final days. Sylvia sometimes thought she'd fallen in love with him then. She felt guilty about that, though her husband had been a difficult and hyper-critical man throughout their thirty year marriage.

She'd told herself many times that her feelings were 'just infatuation', and that they were bound to fade in time.

But still, two years later, here she was, heart beating faster, hoping that Max would not notice her holding her breath as he stood near to her by the altar.

They'd been discussing the music for Easter Sunday, but the organist had long since bustled off and left them to it.

'Would you like to come for lunch after the service?' she asked suddenly, grasping at straws and surprising herself.

Max stared at her. For the first time, he truly noticed her soft grey eyes, the faint flush at the base of her throat, and the way she bit her bottom lip a little when she smiled. He'd only seen her thoughtfulness before. Her sense of humour and her love of music.

'Would you like me to?'

'Yes,' she said, growing bolder. 'I would.'

'Well, in that case.' He felt shy suddenly, stripped of his usual bravado around women. 'Yes, thank you. I'd like that very much.'

-0-0-0-

He was sitting alone in one of the front pews, still wondering what had hit him, when Peter appeared and sat quietly beside him.

'Sorry,' he said. 'Is this a bad time?'

Max shook himself and dragged his musings away from Sylvia Darrowby.

With a sinking heart, he remembered Elin's suspicions about her father.

'Good as any mate,' he said, trying to sound more upbeat than he felt about Peter's sudden presence. 'D'you fancy to come back to the vicarage for a brew?'

-0-0-0-

The vicarage had been built in 1897 by a Church that viewed single vicars with suspicion. The house was large and detached. It had a sizeable garden that Max rarely noticed, and three spare bedrooms that were hardly ever used.

The place was rather too high maintenance for his tastes. He had a cleaner who didn't do much. And a gardener who erred in the opposite direction. Given the choice, he'd have preferred to move a homeless family in and himself out, preferably to a nice low maintenance one bedroom chrome and white town-centre bachelor pad.

Still, beggars can't be choosers, so here he was, in his chintzy sitting room, under the light with bronze cherubs, handing Peter a mug of tea complete with milk and two sugars.

Peter felt so touched that his old bandmate had remembered his 1970's preference that he didn't have the heart to say his tastes had changed. He mentally prepared himself for a sugar rush.

'So,' said Max. 'Have you decided to give us another go then?'

'What? sorry?' Peter was sipping cautiously at his tea.

'The band. Alstrom.'

'Oh... No!'

It seemed strange to Peter, sitting in this old fashioned room, with theology books on the bookshelf, a large, framed print of 'The Hay Wain' on the wall, and a Bible with reading glasses beside it on a stand on the desk.

He stared out of the window to the garden. Looking beyond the red and yellow tulips to a magnolia tree in bloom.

'I guess you're used to hearing people's confessions?' he said suddenly.

Max wondered if Elin had told Peter that she'd spoken to him.

'Not often. It tends to be a more of a group thing in the C of E,' he said, cautiously.

He sat in the fireside chair opposite Peter. 'Why do you ask?'

Peter looked up. Made eye contact. Took a deep breath.

'Because I killed my father,' he said.

Oh fuck! thought Max. What the hell do I do now?

-0-0-0-

'It wasn't deliberate,' said Peter. 'It all happened so quickly. I wasn't thinking straight. And I'd do it differently if I could do it again.'

Max sat opposite quietly. He gazed down at the floor. He was seeking divine inspiration.

'I know I should be telling this to the police. Or Reverend Battersby, at least. He's my local priest after all.'

As the first fog of panic cleared for Max, he remembered the Reverend's 'Day of Judgment' sermon at Isak's funeral. He doubted that anyone ever confessed much of anything to him.

He looked up, determined to do better than that.

'You say it wasn't deliberate,' he said, quietly, surprising himself with how calm he sounded.

Peter ran his hands through his thinning hair, despairing. 'I was just phoning round venues about a possible tour. You remember, I said I'd do that…'

He looked up, seeking confirmation, and Max nodded.

'And I spoke to Arne Karlsson's daughter. She runs a small music venue in Malmö. I thought it would be just about the perfect size for us.... Arne was a saxophonist, a friend of my mother's. She sang with his band at the Nalen jazz club in Stockholm.... Anyway, we got chatting. Her father's ancient of course now, like my own was. He's in a care home. But she mentioned that she'd visited him. That he'd been talking about the European tour he'd done with his band in the Seventies. And how sad it was that my mother was killed just a few weeks before she could join them.'

He took a gulp of tea to try to get rid of the lump in his throat. It didn't work. And it occurred to him that the sugar was almost soapy in his mouth. He'd never noticed that before.

'Dad would never have allowed Mum to go on tour,' he said, seeking an anchor point in Max's gaze. 'I'd always suspected that they must have been arguing the night she died. And that just confirmed it. I went round to confront him. I hadn't seen him since a duty call at Christmas. And before that to tell him that Helen and I had separated.'

Outside, it was starting to rain. Thick drops splattered against the window.

'Anyway,' he continued. 'He was still in his dressing gown and slippers. Said he hadn't been feeling well. He'd had a pounding headache all day. He didn't look ill to me. And I wasn't in the mood to be sympathetic. I just launched straight in with my accusations.'

Across from him, in the fireside chair, Max could sense what was coming.

'I think I must have been quite aggressive about it.'

'He shouted back at first…. *'It was a crazy idea!'* he kept saying. *'I told her it was madness.'* I think now, looking back that maybe he was actually sorry.'

'But you think he caused the accident?'

'Yes, I do! But then, suddenly he got this strange look and staggered back towards his chair. And he sprawled there, half on the chair, and half on the floor. He looked so bewildered. Like he had no idea what was happening. I think he always imagined he was immortal. He was trying to say something. I think he was apologising. But for being ill, not for killing Mum. I couldn't bear to go anywhere near him. I ran and got in the car and locked all the doors, like I was a kid again and scared he'd come after me. I don't know how long passed, But I waited there. It was cold. I turned the car engine on to get warm. And I thought, I could just drive home now. I could pretend I never saw this. But I knew that wasn't the right thing to do. I knew I had to go back and help him. So I forced myself to go back inside. And he'd moved a little, towards the phone, I think. But he was dead.'

-0-0-0-

Max looked across at his old bandmate. He remembered how he'd envied Peter's wealthy lifestyle and glamorous parents. How he'd begrudged him Helen's love and Tyra's devotion. He realised now that he'd never really seen Peter properly at all. And he felt flooded with pity for him.

'You were in shock,' he said, gently. 'You just froze, that's all. No-one can predict how they'll react in circumstances like that.'

'I hated him. I wanted him dead.'

'That's different to killing him.'

'I didn't get help for him.'

Max thought back to all the times he'd wished his own father dead, and how, when the end had finally come, he'd been consumed with grief.

He moved forward and knelt in front of Peter, putting his hand on the sofa next to his old friend's knee. He'd never felt closer to him than he did now.

'Pete,' he said, firmly. 'You have to forgive yourself. You panicked. You went to help him as soon as you were able.'

Peter stared at the floor, consumed by misery.

'Do you think God will forgive me?' he asked.

'I think he already has,' said Max.

Thirty-Four

'Hi Auntie Bridget.'

'Hi Elin, is everything okay?'

'Yes… We're good. And we're really looking forward to our gourmet Easter Sunday lunch with you and Mum at the Five Acres. How are you?'

'I'm fine.'

'Brilliant! I just wanted to talk to you about something. Is this a good time?'

'Sure… Fire away!'

'What's the story with Mum and Tyra?'

'Ah!' Bridget sounded shifty. 'I don't think there *is* a story.'

'So why doesn't Mum want to see her?'

'Oh… *That!*. There was a long pause. Elin figured Bridget was weighing up where her loyalties should lie. With keeping her best friend's secrets. Or with the chance for her to be happy.

'They loved each other,' she said finally. 'They never meant to. But they did. And anyway… It just ended badly, that's all. I don't know all the gory details.'

Elin felt a rush of relief. She'd known this from her very first evening with Tyra on the Spanish mountainside.

'Thank goodness,' she said. 'Now we're finally getting somewhere. How much do you know?'

There was another long silence.

'Your mum *did* love your dad,' she said, eventually, as if she had to somehow validate the union that had produced Elin. 'She had an almighty crush on him when we were at college. I mean… he was so goddamn pretty, even I fancied him…. She'd sussed that if there was an Open Mic night going on, he was likely to be there, singing some soppy love song or another. They got together and she was just, totally smitten for months. But you know he's always been up and down with his moods. And his music has always come first. She ran around after him too much. And I think, in the end, she got tired of it.

It took him ages before he introduced her to his… your… family. And then she was just hook, line and sinker into the whole Alström deal. Gorgeous mum, brooding celebrity dad, talented little sister. Throw in all that Nordic charm, and how could a poor girl from Rotherham resist? Except, of course, the whole place was a house of cards.'

'In what way?' Elin remembered all the times Dave had said similar things. And all the times she'd told him not to be horrible.

'Pretty much every which way really. Your grandma was lovely. I met her several times. She was sweet and kind and bloody beautiful. And she had the voice of an angel. I don't know whether she already had a drink problem before she met Isak, or whether he drove her to it. But you know the level of alcoholism where people never appear drunk, no matter how much they've knocked back? Well, that was Kristina. I imagine she was on tranquillisers as well. Most women were back then. They used to call them 'Happy Pills'. Or 'Mother's Little Helpers'. And the guy she was going out with when she met your grandad.... Arne something or other... He was heavily into heroin for a while.... Though I doubt that Kristina would have held on to her looks like she did if she'd gone down that particular route.

Your grandfather was a tyrant. He ruled the house with a rod of iron. In some warped way, in his own head, I think he may have imagined he was protecting them all. It's hard, you know, living with an addict. Though he was a heavy drinker himself. And boy was he a creep! He came on to me at your mum and dad's wedding. I always suspected that he abused both Tyra and your dad, in different ways. Certainly, he bullied your father incessantly. And Kristina chose not to see it.'

Elin thought of all the times she'd felt uncomfortable around her grandfather. The arguments she'd heard between her parents about whether the kids needed to see him at all. Her mother always reluctant. And her father insisting.

'So how come Mum and Tyra got close?' she asked.

Bridget laughed. 'You've met Tyra,' she said. 'She's so like her mother in personality. Sweet and vulnerable and talented. An addict too, of course. Her parents plied her with alcohol from an early age. And your father got her into tranquillisers. It was the only way she could cope with being centre stage....

Tyra loved your mum from the first moment she saw

her. She told me that, one time, when we…. when we were talking about it…. But for your mum it just never crossed her mind to think like that….. until one day, suddenly, it did.'

Elin digested this.

'Dave's convinced that you and Tyra had a fling,' she said.

'You do all sorts of stupid things when you're young,' said Bridget.

Elin figured that was the closest she'd get to a confession.

'I guess it must have felt impossible for them to be together,' she said. 'Because of Dad, I mean. And the times too. I can't imagine my granny and grandad in Rotherham being over the moon about Mum choosing to be with a woman.'

Bridget laughed. 'They weren't that keen on the Alströms generally to be honest. Fortunately, I don't think they even sussed that Tyra was gay…. Or me for that matter!

But I think your mum would have found a way through all that if Tyra hadn't blamed her for your gran's death. Kristina confided in your mum that she was thinking of going on a tour with Arne What's-his-name and his band. And your mum kept the secret. Tyra thought her parents were probably in the middle of a row about it when the car crashed…. I'm sure it wasn't as simple as that. Your grandma was probably way over the limit too…. Though Tyra and your dad would never have acknowledged that.

So, your mum's basically blamed herself for it all ever since. Especially as Tyra went skidding so dramatically off the rails afterwards. There's no reasoning with her on the subject. God knows, I've tried.

I think she married your father as some kind of a penance for it all. Though…' she added as an afterthought. 'Thank goodness she did, or we wouldn't have you or Fred, or even Lucy.'

They both laughed at the thought of Lucy being a blessing.

Then Elin had an idea. 'Do you think we could guilt-trip Mum into coming to the concert?' she asked.

'I doubt I could keep her away if you said you want her there. Why? It isn't Christmas. You can't string a load of mistletoe over the pair of them you know.'

'Ouch!' Elin cringed as she remembered her clumsy match-making efforts with Bridget and Dave's mum's stepsister. 'I really am sorry about that Auntie B! But, actually, I think I might have a much better idea this time.'

Thirty-Five

FRIDAY 19TH APRIL 2019

The trunk of the hawthorn was gnarled as an old man's arm. It grew at an angle from the scar where Kristina's Alfa Romeo had sliced into the bark, cutting through the arteries of the sapwood, and into the heart of the tree.

Peter ran his hand over it, remembering the pale pulpy softness of the wood that summer after the car had been towed from the ditch. He remembered how the grass of the bank had glistened with jewel-like relics of the car his mother had loved. Red and orange and glinting diamond-like shards from the indicator lights of the caved in front right wing.

Sometimes, when he came here, he would still find these small trophies, eased from the earth, exposed by rain and growing shoots. He'd always taken them home with him. He had a pencil box his mother had given him. He'd kept them there to keep her memory close.

Today, he'd placed the box at the base of the tree. He'd brought flowers. White lilies. His mother's favourite. There was a vase beside the tree where he always left them. He'd never been able to bear just leaving them to die in cellophane beside the road.

He felt the old familiar grief rising within him. But more intense on this final visit.

'I'm sorry Mum, I can't do this anymore,' he said, kissing his hand and placing it against the rough bark of the tree.

He looked up at the sky, which was a perfect, pastel blue. The colour of a sweater she'd bought him once, in one of those precious fleeting times when he was happy.

Slowly, he walked back to his car.

-0-0-0-

In her Airbnb flat in the old asylum, Tyra tried to shake the anxiety she'd felt all day. She'd woken from her old familiar nightmares, and, at first she'd thought her unease was just a hangover from that. She'd learnt over the years that distraction was the best strategy. Brooding too much never ended well. And attempts to medicate the pain only served to postpone it. She'd volunteered to walk Dido, thinking that fresh air and exercise would do her good. But the sense of unease lingered after the dog was returned and snoring peacefully in her basket at home.

She found that she couldn't get Peter out of her mind. Or her mother. She thought this must have been triggered by her brother's visit the day before. Or being so close now to Renton Hall. But the memories felt like torture. Images of birthdays, Christmases, trips to the seaside and lakes in Sweden and here in the UK. Just the three of them, happy without Isak. She wondered how her father must have felt being excluded like that. The vicious spiralling of his anger. And how trapped her mother must have felt by her love for him.

-0-0-0-

It was a quiet road. And the layby was secluded. It was the kind of place couples might park, away from prying eyes. Someone had fly-tipped an old mattress at the far end. Springs and wisps of coir fibre escaped from its torn satin-white casing.

A tractor rumbled by, and then everything was quiet. Peter had run the hosepipe along the passenger side of his father's beloved vintage Bentley. He was aware of the unconscious symbolism in his choice. Though he'd chosen the Bentley initially because he had no idea how to remove the catalytic convertor from his own Ford Focus at home.

On his phone there was a text message from Lucy. 'I think I've found the perfect place for us Dad.'

He didn't have the energy to reply.

He wondered in a hazy kind of way, what would happen to the Bentley after it had killed him. He wasn't sure people would want to drive it after that. And the thought made him feel sad. Isak had always lavished so much more love on it than he had on his son. It had suited his image to arrive at village events in that grand old aristocrat of a car. But Peter had grown quite fond of it too, as a ghostly companion, covered in dust sheets when he was banished to the coach house with his violin.

The sound of his phone vibrating on the seat, face down

beside him was annoying. It kept stopping. And then starting again. Like a beggar on a city street, who wouldn't take 'No' for an answer.

Blurrily, he flipped the phone over, fumbling to find the 'off' switch, and saw Tyra's name where he had expected to see Lucy's.

He figured she'd be much easier to fob off than his daughter ever was.

'Hi,' he said, not realising how groggy he sounded.

'Pete,' she gasped, flooded with relief at getting him. 'Are you okay? You don't sound okay.' And then, subconsciously remembering the idling purr of the Bentley from her youth. 'Turn the engine off now. And open the door. Where are you? I'm coming. Now!'

-0-0-0-

The taxi driver seemed unfazed at cruising the country lanes around Renton Hall. Maybe he helped lots of people locate cars in remote laybys in the middle of the Essex countryside.

He seemed proud of himself when he spotted the Bentley and pulled in behind it.

Tyra tipped him generously and ran to Peter, who was sitting on the driver's seat of the car, door open, slumped forward, with his elbows on his knees and his feet planted firmly on the stony ground.

'Are you okay?' she asked again. She felt relieved that now, at least, she could make that judgment for herself.

He shook his head like someone with the mother of all hangovers.

She knelt beside him and wrapped her arms around his shoulders touching her forehead against his. It was a throwback to when they were young and Isak had been shouting at him. An ancient gesture of solidarity from when the dust had settled and she'd dare to track him down, in the coach house, or in his room, or hiding somewhere in the garden.

'Why?' she asked.

'I'm sick of people pitying me,' he said.

She took off her jacket and put it on the damp ground so she could sit beside him, resting her head against his knee.

'It'll get dirty,' said Peter.

'It doesn't matter. I've got a washing machine back at the flat.'

She looked up at the blue sky, darkening a little now, as the afternoon wore on.

Then she glanced across the road to where the crooked hawthorn stood.

'Is that the place?' she asked. She'd never wanted to come here, unlike Peter, with his regular pilgrimages to the spot.

He nodded, and she shivered involuntarily, picturing it.

'Do you ever wonder if she did it on purpose?' she asked. It was an idea that had come to her slowly, as she put time and space between herself and the events of that fateful time. 'Like maybe, in a moment of madness, she thought it was the only way out for her.'

Peter shook his head. 'She'd never do that to us,' he said. 'She loved us too much.'

'And you don't love Elin... or Fred... or Lucy?' She looked up at him and saw him flinch.

'They don't need me anymore.'

'Like we didn't need Mum?'

He shut up and stroked his hand over her hair, like he used to when she was still his little sister.

'She was no saint Peter. You do know that don't you? No-one is. Though we all imagined she was at the time.'

He didn't answer. But she knew that he understood what she was saying.

'I can't cope with it anymore,' he said. 'It's all too much for me. This. You. Helen. The kids. Lucy wants me to live with her in a 'grandad flat' in Sweden, for God's sake.'

Tyra laughed at this, 'Well, their quality of life for 'seniors' is second to none.'

'God, you sound like Lucy. It makes me feel like Methuselah.'

'Come back to the band then. Be a recycled teenager. Grow old disgracefully.'

He shook his head. It wasn't an option. He knew that now.

'No, the band was already growing away from me back in the seventies. Brian was still on the same page... more or less... But you'd changed... And Max and Danny always preferred the other stuff.'

They fell into silence, staring down at the ground, hearing the soft hum of a distant road, the wind stirring the hedge behind them.

A blackbird plucked padding from the fly-tipped mattress.

'I need to get away,' said Peter. 'I can't bear my life here anymore. I need to draw a line under it somehow.'

Tyra felt swamped with loneliness at that, feeling that she'd found her brother, only to lose him again.

'Well, I know a good place in Spain,' she said.

-0-0-0-

Lucy screamed in frustration when Peter phoned to tell her he wouldn't be moving to Sweden.

'I suppose you're getting back with Mum!' she stormed. 'I *knew* you would! You must be *mad* after the way she's treated you!'

Peter chose not to bother enlightening her.

Fred didn't mind much either way. England or Sweden or Spain were all transatlantic flights for him. And he doubted he'd miss someone he rarely saw anyway.

Elin hid her tears throughout the call. 'Can I come see you?' she asked.

'Maybe, when I'm settled. I'll write.'

-0-0-0-

It was easy to pack. He'd left everything in perfect order.

He hadn't wanted people to judge him after he'd gone.

Tyra helped him out of the house with the few items he'd need in the less-encumbered life he was choosing.

He put the key into an envelope with a letter addressed to his solicitor.

'He'll deal with everything,' he said. 'They'll be open on

Tuesday after the Bank Holiday. Are you okay with taking it and leaving it with his receptionist?'

'Of course. No problem.'

He hugged her tightly, as he used to when he went away to school and she was still young enough to stay at home. And she found herself clinging to him, as she had then, forcing her adult self, in the end, to let him go.

She waved until he was out of sight. And stood motionless until she could no longer hear the engine of the car. Finally, when all trace of him was gone, she allowed herself to cry.

Thirty-Six

FRIDAY 3ᴿᴰ MAY 2019

'Rats in the Stairwell' were big in their native Essex. And their latest tour of the UK had been a triumph.

The atmosphere at the 950 seater King's Hall was buzzing.

It was a beautiful 'listed' Edwardian Theatre House, and the plush red seats had not quite enough leg room for the taller modern concert goer. The ornate carvings along the balcony were picked out in gold, and chandeliers hung and sparkled from the ceiling. Satie's Gymnopédies played discretely as the audience wandered in from the bar. It was possibly a risky venue for a heavy metal band's homecoming. Though the 'Rats' fans were renowned for being immaculately well behaved.

Helen felt nauseous. She told herself that this was due to vicarious nerves for Elin, who surely, must be daunted by the size of this place. Secretly, she knew she was also terrified at the thought of seeing Tyra again. There was going to be an after-gig get-together, of course. And she didn't see how she could avoid it without hurting her daughter.

She was seated in the fifth row of the stalls. Dave had been busily chatting to a few friends who'd come to offer Elin moral support. But now he'd settled himself on her right hand side. And Bridget was to her left. She wondered if they'd hemmed her in deliberately so she couldn't bolt.

It felt strange being there, especially as she'd picked out several clusters of kids from her old school. They were fans of the headline act, clearly. The ones who spotted her waved politely. She'd been Deputy Head after all. And she hoped her presence wouldn't get in the way of them enjoying themselves. But they treated Dave like a favourite uncle, waving and mouthing (and in some cases, outright yelling), 'Hello Sir', across the auditorium at him.

In this heavy metal audience with their denim and leather, Helen felt she had been transported back to the days when she was 'with the band'. Though the atmosphere wasn't smoky like it used to be. And the drinks were in plastic glasses now, so the performers wouldn't get injured if the audience got bored and resorted to throwing things at them.

On stage, four young lads were busily setting up and checking Alstrom's equipment. Dave whispered that they were 'modern apprentices', from Danny's studio. Helen was glad to see that they seemed to know what they were doing.

Looking around, she'd been relieved to see a scattering of Alstrom fans too, identifiable by their age, or lack of heavy metal uniform, or even, in a few instances, by original T-shirts, screen printed lovingly by Peter, when he still had dreams of making it to the big time. She thought it was fortunate that the traditional Alstrom colours had always been purple on grey. Colours that could weather the yellowing of time. Some appeared to have brought their teenage grandkids with them. Some were alone. And there was a gathering of about twenty, at the front, that looked like it might have been organised by the Alstrom Fan Group on Facebook.

Satie stopped abruptly. The house lights dimmed. Stewards in fluorescent jackets moved to the sides and front of the house.

The band filed on stage. And the front row fans leapt out of their seats and surged to greet them, hands in the air, clapping and cheering and whistling at the return of their long lost heroes.

The stewards shrugged and decided they were probably harmless.

Light swept the stage, and a huge cheer went up again for the original members of the band. Max, in a Hawaiian style shirt and baggy cargoes, his hair tied back in a ponytail. Danny, in red, green, and gold, already deep in his performance trance. And Tyra, all in black, hiding in the shadows, where she preferred to be.

The ominous rumble of her keyboard filled the auditorium.

The spotlight swung back to Elin as she stepped up to the microphone.

'Go Elin!' yelled Dave, leaping to his feet in his excitement, and drawing giggles from his students, who joined in with his enthusiasm, yelling 'Go Mrs Dave!'

She smiled out into the shadowy depths of the audience.

'Hello Essex,' she said. 'Do you know Stonewall is Coming?'

-0-0-0-

Tyra hadn't expected to miss Peter as much as she did. She was touched by the gesture someone (probably Elin) had made, propping a guitar and violin against one of the amps to the left of the stage, where he would have stood. But she still felt an absence where his golden presence should have been. Without his baroque flourishes, the songs were stripped down, sparer. She wondered if the fans would like them like that. She missed him most in 'Beowulf', always his favourite, and the beginning of the unravelling between them.

She had the Set List Blu-tacked to the monitor beside her, though she knew it off by heart.

'Stonewall', 'Beowulf', then 'Mad House Reggae'…. 'Sod Off with Your Sympathy', their only excursion into punk…. And 'Going Down'. They were going to include the new song she'd written on the day of her father's funeral too. And then The Fördömelse Theme, of course. And another new song, 'Where Dreams Come to Die,' if they were lucky enough to be asked for an encore.

That was plenty. They didn't want to hog the limelight of the home coming 'Rats', or test their own stamina, or memories, for too long.

And it seemed to be going well. The fans were happy to have them back, chanting and singing along at the front, while Dave kept up his enthusiastic cheerleading from the fifth row.

She was preparing to launch into 'Fördömelse' when Elin jolted her by diverting from the planned programme.

'I was out walking my dog the other day,' she said. 'And I heard my aunt writing a song. I figured she was planning on keeping it under wraps. But I thought the words were too important for that. So, me and the band have been practising in secret…. And Tyra…. You already know how this goes… I hope you'll join in, because I'm going to feel a bit daft if you don't.'

She shaded her eyes and peered out towards the fifth row.

'Mum, I think this one's for you.'

-0-0-0-

The gilded theatre spun as Helen took in Tyra's words of loss and longing.

Hesitant at first, and then stronger, Tyra's playing joined Max and Danny's, holding up Elin's pure vocals, as they soared out over the auditorium.

Then both Alstrom women were singing. Tyra providing the harmonies to Elin's lead.

Helen's eyes blurred with tears. Bridget put her hand on her arm to steady her.

And even Dave was crying, though he was pretending not to.

Thirty-Seven

TWO MONTHS LATER

Summer sunshine was streaming into Helen's bedroom. It lit up tiny dancing dust motes, and made her vow that she must do a proper 'spring clean' while Tyra was away on tour. She hadn't had time for such things recently. There had been too many lost years. And now each moment together was precious.

Tyra wandered in from the bathroom, towelling her hair. She came over to kiss Helen good morning.

'So,' she said, laughing. 'You're awake at last.'

'Mm…. It was nice to sleep in. I was tired. Some sexy woman kept me up half the night.'

'Really? You'd better tell me who she is right now, so I can go fight her.'

Helen laughed and cupped Tyra's face in her hands. 'God, you're so gorgeous,' she said. 'I can't believe you're about to abandon me again.'

'I know!' Tyra grimaced. 'I don't know why I even agreed

to it. But the band were so thrilled at the thought of 'doing' Europe. I didn't have the heart to let them down this time.'

Helen thought of her daughter, and how much she was looking forward to the tour.

'Yes,' she admitted. 'Elin's beside herself with excitement. Dave's a bit woebegone though. And Dido will probably have a complete doggy breakdown with both you and Elin away. I'll have to drop in regularly with home cooking for Dave and treats and tummy tickles for the dog.'

She unconsciously ruffled her fingers through Tyra's hair as she said it.

Tyra laughed.

'That should do the trick. It always works for me. Will you miss me?'

'God, sweetheart, I can't even begin to tell you how much. Though it might be quite nice to have my bathroom back. You take longer than any of the kids did, even when they were teenagers.'

Tyra laughed apologetically. 'I'm sorry! It's the Power Shower. I'm addicted to it. Some of the places I've dossed down over the past few years have been basic, to say the least. The one at the Airbnb's pretty clunky too. And I imagine the next couple of months aren't exactly going to be luxurious…. But I've been thinking. I got talking to your neighbour upstairs a couple of days ago. She asked me if I was your sister… I wasn't sure whether she was being euphemistic or not. So I didn't 'out' you. But she mentioned that she's going to be moving. And I wondered if you'd think I was being scarily intrusive if I rented her flat. It would be nice to live closer to you. I wouldn't need to hog your shower... Unless you fancy to get in there with me, of course... And I'm going to have to move out of that Airbnb anyway. Me and the wallpaper are having an Oscar Wilde style 'dual to the death'...'

She stopped, scanning Helen's face for her response. She'd tried to keep it light-hearted, but she knew she'd feel rejected if she saw any doubt there.

She was relieved to see her lover's face light up. 'Are you kidding me? I'd love it! What a perfect idea. We'd be under the same roof but with plenty of space when we need it. I'll talk to the landlord if you like, I can't imagine it would be easy for you to arrange from abroad.'

Tyra breathed a sigh of relief.

'Great! You're a star. Now you just stay right there while I go make us some brunch.'

-0-0-0-

'You'll never guess who I saw on Facebook while you were making this.'

They were propped on pillows, on the bed. Mugs of Tyra's richly brewed coffee steamed on the bedside cabinets beside them. Helen scrolled to the 'Alstrom Fan Group' on her phone and handed it to Tyra.

'There!' she said, pointing to the top post. 'The video with the comment, 'Look who I spotted in Granada.'

Tyra tapped on it.

She recognised the rectangular Plaza Larga. The sun was shining. And the sky was a vivid blue. It was probably lunchtime. The tables outside the whitewashed cafés and bars were full. Peter wore baggy shorts and sandals, a massive white T-shirt, and an unkempt beard that made him look like a sixties hippy. He looked tanned and healthy and unusually relaxed, with his violin tucked under his chin and a small portable boombox providing a distinctly Alstromesque backing. He was playing 'Rondo Alla Turkish Delight,' the final movement of Mozart's Piano Sonata Number 11, adapted in his inimitable style, for violin and rock band. He seemed to be in his own world in that bustling place, his fingers flying effortlessly over the strings as if they belonged to the instrument. Tyra remembered how he was always at his most peaceful when he was playing. But there was something else about him there. He looked happy. And he looked free.

She watched, transfixed, as he came to the end of the piece and posed with the photographer, smiling and winking into the camera. Tyra sensed that he knew they would see it.

'It's lovely isn't it?' said Helen. She'd rested her head against Tyra's shoulder to watch it again with her.

Tyra felt her eyes brimming with tears of relief.

Helen saw and took the phone from her.

'Come here!' She took her in her arms and held her for a long time. 'He's okay now,' she said. 'Thank goodness.'

Tyra nodded and rubbed her eyes on the back of her hand.

'I wonder if the band have seen this.'

'They certainly have!' Helen showed Tyra the heart Elin had put on the clip, and the more 'manly' likes from Max and Danny. 'And speaking of the band... What time is Max picking you up?'

Tyra glanced at her watch. It was 12 o'clock already. Time was running away towards this new, but very different goodbye to Helen.

'12.45,' she said glumly.

Helen thought of all the wasted years. The loneliness. And the guilt. She told herself that this time it was different. Tyra would come home. Back to this house. Back into her arms.

For a moment, she felt frightened, not sure of any of that anymore.

'You will come home, won't you?' she asked, needing to know that it was true..

'Wild horses couldn't stop me!'

Helen nodded, reassured by the honesty she'd always seen in Tyra's eyes.

'Are you all packed?'

'Yes. Everything's in the hall and ready to load into the van.'

'Is there anything else you need to do?'

'Well, only the usual… You know… Getting dressed and stuff.'

Helen knew that would take Tyra all of five minutes.

'In that case,' she whispered. 'Please… Will you hold me till it's time for you to go?'

THE END

Jane Retzig is a U.K based author.
Her full length novels are...

Boundaries
The Full Legacy
The Photograph
The Wrong Woman
A Question of Trust
A Betrayal
A Perfect Storm
The Retreat
A Tale of Two Sisters
Alstrom

Jane also created the music of Alstrom.

Her email is: janeretzig@gmail.com
Her website is www.janeretzig.com

tning Source UK Ltd.
Keynes UK
20829060223
X00016B/1843